... stories have appeared in ... literary magazines and journals. He won the 2018 *Riptide Journal* short story competition, was runner-up in the 2019 Leicester Writes competition, and was highly commended in the Manchester Writing School competition 2018. He is also co-author of a comic novel-in-emails about an eccentric writers' group, *Kitten on a Fatberg* (Unbound).

He lives in London with his partner Eve and their three children – Isla, Poppy and Huw.

BY THE SAME AUTHOR

Kitten on a Fatberg (Co-author, Unbound)

HOTEL DU JACK

AND OTHER STORIES

DAN BROTZEL

SANDSTONE PRESS

First published in Great Britain by
Sandstone Press Ltd
Willow House
Stoneyfield Business Park
Inverness
IV2 7PA
Scotland

www.sandstonepress.com

Copyright © Dan Brotzel 2020
Editor: Moira Forsyth

The moral right of Dan Brotzel to be recognised as the
author of this work has been asserted in accordance with
the Copyright, Designs and Patents Act 1988.

This is a work of fiction. Names, characters, businesses, places, events
and incidents are either the products of the author's imagination
or used in a fictitious manner. Any resemblance to actual persons,
living or dead, or actual events is purely coincidental.

The publisher acknowledges subsidy from Creative
Scotland towards publication of this volume.

Printed   Y

For Eve

CONTENTS

NOTHING SO BLUE

I'm not sure of all the technical details. I can only tell you it's not all it's cracked up to be, it really isn't. Plus I made a crap choice. Why didn't I just go for flying, like a normal person?

Basically, what happened was that we were all in the pub after work, and we were talking about Cal, our divisional head. Cal's on his third wife, and has just announced they're having a kid (to go with the ones he's got from each of his previous marriages). I also remember it was pissing down outside.

Lynne, our team leader, who's been trying to get pregnant for ever, said Cal was the sort of bloke who only had to look at a woman to get her pregnant.

'It's his superpower,' I think I said, which got a bit of a laugh.

'I wish it was mine,' said Lynne.

And then we got into one of those stupid pub conversations about superpowers, and which one you'd choose. Zoe and a few others went for flying, of course, although Arvi, who's a mad diver, said he'd want to be able to breathe underwater. I said I'd like to be invisible for a day, I don't know why. I remember there was thunder and lightning, and for a few moments the lights in the pub flickered. It looked dark and wet outside, an excuse to stay on for an extra drink or two.

Karen said she'd like the ability to have the perfect comeback for every occasion, while Tommo said his superpower was already well-known among the ladies of his acquaintance. *Hurhurhrr*, said the lads present. *Ew*, said me and all the other women.

There followed a discussion of the relative merits of teleportation and super-speed. Jav opted for the latter: he said that if you could move that fast you'd also have to be endowed with the ability to think just as fast too, which would mean you could absorb all the world's information and become incredibly educated and enlightened, and so able to lead society to a better and juster future. Someone else said that extra powers would just mean more ways for people to get whatever they wanted.

Tania, still thinking, couldn't decide if she wanted to look good in any outfit she wore, or to be able to understand cats perfectly. That of course got everyone on to sharing cat videos, and the superpower discussion was over.

Except that, when I woke next morning and stretched out for my phone, I noticed that I couldn't see my arm.

I stumbled into the bathroom, looked in the mirror, and just couldn't see myself. At first I thought it had to be a trick of the light. In the murk of dawn the shadow of the door casts a reflection on the mirror, and I thought somehow that this was obscuring the reflection of me. This makes no sense, of course, but when you've just become invisible, you're ready to believe all sorts of things that don't really make any sense but are slightly more plausible than the idea that you have just become invisible.

I switched the bathroom light on, and I was blatantly *not there*. I shone a torch at the mirror. Nothing. I ran round the flat, looking for more mirrors. I took selfies in which I didn't appear, and stared at the results. The camera just looked right through me. I wandered round the flat in a daze, trying to process what had happened.

I tried to reach my brother but his phone went to message. I couldn't think of anyone else to call who'd take me seriously. There was Jed, my alleged boyfriend, but he and I were on a sort of break yet again, and the last time we'd seen each other we'd had another massive row. Ironically, I think I actually accused him of treating me like I was invisible.

I wanted to reach my mum, of course, but there's not much to reach there now.

It probably sounds ridiculous but my next thought was to dial 111. I got about thirty seconds into my explanation before I sensed the call was taking a wrong turn.

'Are you bleeding at all, Katya? How does your heart feel?'

'Fine. Nothing else is wrong with me! I just can't . . . *be seen.*'

'OK, I see.' There was a pause, as if the operator was switching scripts. 'And how have you been feeling in yourself recently?'

'Fine, fine! I'm a bit hungover but only 'cos we went to the pub last night.'

'I see. Now . . . have you had trouble sleeping at all recently?'

'No.'

'Do you ever feel that you've let other people down?'

Only by being granted an actual superpower wish and having such a crap time with it, I wanted to say.

'Not at all, no. I'm fine,' I actually said.

She asked some questions about my appetite, and energy levels, and whether I had trouble concentrating on things.

'Well, I work in payroll,' I replied. 'I spend most of my time being shouted at by people who think it's my fault there's money missing from their pay. I think anyone would struggle to feel energised and excited about that all the time.'

This got me thinking. What was I going to do about work today?

'I see. And have you had any unhelpful thoughts?'

'Well, I wished I was invisible, didn't I? As I explained already. That's turned out to be pretty unhelpful so far.' As I spoke, I was shaking talc onto my arms. I could see their outline at last, albeit in a powdery, diaphanous kind of way.

'Right, yes. I meant more, have you had the urge to hurt yourself or others?'

Oh crap. I could see where this was going.

'No, no. Actually! I'm starting to feel a whole lot better! Thanks so much for talking to me, you've really calmed me down! I think I must have just over-indulged last night . . .'

I managed to talk myself out of the call, hopefully in a way that wouldn't have the men in white coats banging the door down.

I emailed work. *Sorry Lynne, but can't make it in today. Been throwing up all night – think it's that bug that's been going round.*

Pulling a sickie was easier when I had a male boss. With Cal, when he was just our humble team leader, all it took was some dark reference to 'ladies' troubles' and he'd be off the phone like a shot. But there always *is* a bug going round, isn't there? And anyway, I couldn't possibly go in. I wasn't ill exactly, but I was certainly *indisposed.*

I made some tea but I had no milk. I'd been round at Jed's a lot recently, and there wasn't much food in either. This seemed as good a moment as any to venture outside.

I slipped on some sandals, a pair of jeans and a T-shirt, and stepped out. But the reaction I got from people as soon as I hit the street was drastic. People saw this mad headless life-size scarecrow ragdoll thing striding down the road and they frankly shat themselves. Some cowered in doorways; some tried to shield their children; some stood stock still, as if playing dead. One bloke just legged it down the road.

Fortunately it was still early so there weren't too many about. But the ones I ran into were so shocked *they didn't even get their phones out.*

In retrospect I should perhaps have expected this re-action. After all, I was still pretty freaked myself. I retreated back to the flat and checked out my appearance again in the long wardrobe mirror. I was a sight. Well, sort of.

I put down some biscuits for Lulu. No need for her to go hungry. She sniffed my airspace suspiciously, but she didn't do her normal little chirpy yelp of greeting. It choked me to think that even my cat couldn't recognise me. Who knew being invisible would feel so lonely?

When you ask people what they'd do if they became in-visible, they talk about righting the world's wrongs, or going to all the places they've never been before, or living out vari-ous cheesy erotic fantasies (Tommo). But you never hear about the practicalities. Far from luxuriating in my in-credible new power, I was finding the most basic functions of life almost impossible.

The fact is, for example, that although *you* are invisible, nothing else is. So if you really wanted to walk about the world undetected, you'd actually have to be *naked*, which is both chilly and very hard on the feet. And as you don't know when (or if) the invisibility 'spell' will wear off, you are basic-ally running the constant risk of exposing yourself.

I did think of stripping off, tiptoeing down to the corner shop and nicking a few bits. You're virtually obliged to steal things when you're invisible, it seemed to me. After all, how can you pay for stuff? You could leave cash on the counter when no one's looking, I suppose, but how would you carry money about in the first place? Your purse or handbag would just float in the air – as would your pint of milk and tin of beans. You can't move anything about without freaking people out.

Except in your mouth, I suppose. If I didn't want to alarm people, I suppose I could sneak naked to the shops with a fiver clamped inside my gob. But I'd have to only buy very small things I could also carry in my mouth, like stamps or penny chews. And what if someone saw these things suddenly appearing or disappearing? Perhaps the only thing weirder than a fiver floating unaided across Tesco's is a floating fiver that suddenly dematerialises as if swallowed by an invisible orifice.

I was actually experimenting with putting different things in my mouth and looking in the mirror, when I realised that I could of course just conceal small things in a clenched hand instead. Which just shows you how I was losing the ability to think straight.

As for using your superpower to go wherever you want, don't forget you've still got to *get there*. Imagine suddenly re-materialising in mid-air on your flight to Rio. Where would you have been sitting on the plane all that time anyway? Or would you have been standing naked in the aisle? You may be invisible but you still *take up space*.

It'd be the same problem if you wanted to sneak into places unseen: you'd have to squeeze against walls and avoid places with too many people in, so they didn't bump into you and freak. Life would become a kind of weird variation of blind man's buff, with everyone else blind to you, and you in the buff. What if I slipped in to Buck House and was secretly observing Meghan and the Queen having a row about breast-feeding over breakfast, but then Harry does a big yawn and accidentally sticks a finger in my nose? I wouldn't know where to look. And nor, of course, would he.

*

6

In this way I tried to make light of things for myself, but it really wasn't very funny. The reaction of people outside had really alarmed me. I kept thinking of that film *The Elephant Man*, which Jed and I had watched recently. Now *I* was the monster, and I felt horribly vulnerable. I felt sure that once people had got over the shock of my invisibility, they would want to trap me and exploit me. Look at John Merrick, look at ET, look at *The Man from Atlantis*. It's always the way.

Then I remembered that Merrick went about in a big black cloak with a cap and a sort of sack over his head. I still needed to get out and get some food, so I decided this time to cover up as best as I could. Not being a skier, a bank robber or a paramilitary insurgent, I had no balaclava to hand, but I did what I could. I wore long boots with thick heels, jeans (not ripped ones, obviously), a pair of thin gloves, and a long-sleeve rollie with a high neck which I stretched out as far as I could, right up to the underside of my chin. I rubbed a load of talc in my face, and covered as much as possible of the space where my head should have been with a dark scarf and a sweat top with the hood up.

In the mirror, I could see I looked no better than before. My face was ghostly pale and you couldn't see my eyes, which were stinging a bit from all that talc. I looked a bit like the Night King in *Game of Thrones*. It was a boiling hot August day too, and within seconds I was sweating like a dog.

It was ridiculous really. No one could see me, yet I still had to hide myself from view.

I sped along the street in an anonymous shuffle, head down and eyes forward. Now that I was actually out, I thought I might as well get as much stuff in as I could. (If this invisibility thing continued, I could see myself doing a lot of online shopping.) So I walked past the corner shop and all the way up to the big Asda, where I whizzed round and picked up a load of basic food bits, five big tubs of talc and – on a sudden inspiration – a load of foundation and skin stuff. I might end up looking like Donald Trump, I decided, but at least I'd look like *something*.

As I was debating with myself about skin tones, a kindly assistant came over.

'Can I help you with anything . . . sir?'

Sir? I think I knew what she was thinking. Here was this odd-looking 'bloke' nervously eyeing up makeup. Clearly I was a questioning trans, and she, bless her, was keen to put me at my ease. She wanted me to know that she did not judge me in any way. I was in need of a bit of kindness right then, and she was so obviously well-meaning that I looked up, gave her a big smile and met her eyes.

Mistake. The look she gave me back was one of pure horror. I suppose the living dead have that effect on people.

I hate the self-service machines as a rule because they do people out of work, but they were a great option this time. I scurried over and scanned my items as fast as I could, albeit not too fast as I was desperate not to make a mistake and have to call the supervisor over. I bagged up my stuff and headed out the door. Through the window I saw the woman from the make-up aisle in a huddle with some co-workers over by the pharmacy counter. They kept staring at each other, and then at me.

It was oppressive being out and about, when you feel defined by one aspect of your identity (admittedly one that defies all known laws of science), and you feel you could be found out for it at any moment, stared at, ostracised, perhaps even attacked. I wanted to shout: *I am more than just my super-power!* But the whole world had become a scary estate, and I was the kid in the ludicrous purple private-school blazer and straw boater, walking through mean streets where I didn't belong.

To escape the outside world quicker I decided to get the bus back, but not before slipping down a little alley and rubbing a load more talc into my face. I'd just finished when a washed-out-looking bloke came up to me and asked if I had any *white* or *beans* or *blues*. These weren't words I was familiar with in context, but I got the general idea. I said that I was sorry I couldn't help him.

'Safe,' said the man, and we bumped fists at his invitation. As we did so, I saw that half his bottom teeth were missing and there was a nasty carbuncle thing on his neck that was clearly a stranger to the amoxicillin. And yet after he'd melted away I felt a sudden pang, because he had treated me like a normal person, and he had been the only one.

The bus was busy, but people still gave me a wide berth. I stood by the door, ready to jump off at the next stop if things got out of hand. It was a relief to get back into the flat with my groceries and to close the door on the world.

So: what's being invisible like, you ask? Well, it's like no one can see you. It's like you can't even see yourself. And that's about it. Nothing else changes. My mum is still in a home, on a one-way road to silence and fear. I'm still terrified of speaking in public. I still hate my job, and I'm still jealous of Jed's ex, even though I'm not even sure we're together any more. Lynne still can't get pregnant. Nigel Farage still exists. The laws of physics still apply in all their other dull and predictable respects. I haven't got any braver or cleverer or kinder. Dresses still don't have enough pockets. And I still loathe my fringe, although at least now I don't have to look at it, thank God.

Lynne emailed from work. She said that half the team hadn't turned up today. *What's got into everyone?* Apparently, Arvi had called a duvet day and said he was heading for the coast. The only ones who'd made it in were Tania, who incidentally kept changing her clothes and looked absolutely amazing in everything; Karen, who'd had everyone in stitches all day; and Tommo, who was just Tommo.

I was starting to wonder if I wasn't the only one who'd been endowed with a superpower when I heard a tapping at my kitchen window. A very definite persistent knocking, like a human knuckle on glass – which is kind of surprising when you consider that I live on the third floor.

There they were, two of my colleagues, hovering fifty feet off the ground. One was Zoe, and I didn't know the other very well. Siobhan, was it, or Shelley? She'd only been here a week or two, and it seemed a bit rich that she was getting to fly when she was still on probation and couldn't even work the annual-leave allocation system yet.

'Katya!' called Zoe, delirious.

'Hello there,' said the other one stiffly.

'Hi Zoe!' I called back to Zoe. 'Good morning,' I said to the other one, who just nodded. It was obvious that neither of us could remember the other's name. Even though Sheila or Shona or whoever was currently balanced in an elegant, gravity-defying arabesque on a chimney pot and I was a translucent talc-spattered spectre, there was still a certain formality between us.

'Come and join us, Katya!' shouted Zoe now. 'It's *amazing!*'

'So you got your wish!' I said stupidly. 'But how do you do it?'

'I don't know!' Zoe called back. 'I just woke up and knew I could fly! Come on – join us!'

'I can't,' I said. 'I chose invisibility.' I had never felt less like someone who could fly in my life.

'But I can see you!' said Zoe. 'Well, a bit. You look awful.'

'Help me,' I called back mournfully. 'How long do you think this is going to last?'

'Oh my God! Let's just hope . . . forever!' whooped Zoe, doing an amazing loop-the-loop. 'I'm flying, Katya! I'm *freeeeeeeeeee!*'

And she was gone. I couldn't blame her. If that was my superpower I probably wouldn't give a flying fuck about anything else either.

The same thing was probably happening with Jav. He was probably too busy running up and down mountains to stop and think about saving civilisation. And of course Arvi would doubtless be dancing with an octopus or mating with a stingray right now.

No one, after all, had asked for kindness or thoughtfulness as their superpower. I hadn't either; if I'm honest, the only reason I'd said invisibility was to be different from Zoe and that new girl, who'd both said flying. I didn't want people to think I was a cliché; how sad is that?

But whereas all the others were terrified their power would stop, I was living under a terrible shadow of dread that none of this would ever end.

I spent the afternoon eating, watching crap TV, and trying not to trip up or bump myself on my unseen limbs (harder than you might think). I think I wept a bit. I recall that I crawled under my duvet. I may also have opened a bottle of Chardonnay.

(By the way, in case you're wondering, I cast no shadow. How could I? I reflected no light.)

As I was about to pour another glass of wine, I remembered something my mum used to say. 'Every problem is just an adventure in disguise! Where will yours take you today?'

You can probably tell she used to be an art teacher. I'm not sure how that philosophy is working for her now, now she can barely speak or eat, and spends her days staring out of the window or shouting *He'll be here on Tuesday!* over and over, for hours on end.

But I must have been gripped by a sudden urge to make the most of my situation, because I put the wine bottle down. Another glass would put me over the limit. Why would an invisible person worry about driving offences, you ask? Well, for starters, it was still my car. There was nothing invisible about my mustard-coloured Corsa and if I crashed I'd still bleed, even if the paramedics couldn't see my blood.

I'd told myself I wouldn't, I'd promised myself not to. But I did. I got back into my Night King gear and drove over to Jed's. In the car I stripped off my clothes and slipped into his back garden through the gate he never locked properly.

Jed wasn't there, of course; he was at work. But through the patio window I saw Jane, his air-quote *ex*. Jane, who was in his brown dressing gown and had her hair up in a towel, seemed very much at home. (I recognised her from Sainsbury's, where she worked as a supervisor.) As I watched, she strolled into the kitchen, bent down and put some washing on.

My heart beat hard. I felt sick and wobbly. But there was a kind of relief too. For months I'd been suspicious about Jed and his feelings for Jane. It was the way he tried never to mention her name or became guarded and evasive if I ever brought her up.

I'd been right to be suspicious, to wonder if he still had feelings for her. But I didn't need to worry any more, because now I just *knew*. Maybe this was a new thing, provoked by our latest break-up, or maybe it was a long-running affair. In the scheme of things, it didn't really matter. Now at least I knew where I stood.

I'm making it sound like I was calm and philosophical about the whole thing, but I really wasn't. That's probably why I ran round the house, tapping on the patio window and then on the kitchen window and then on the front door. Jane looked up, alarmed. She kept wheeling round, to try and see where each new noise was coming from. As I watched, she got more and more frantic. Poor love.

Then I started picking up bits of garden furniture and causing them to 'levitate' around the garden. I made chairs spin and fat-balls loop-the-loop. When the bird table apparently lifted itself onto the big patio table, I saw Jane run upstairs screaming. But floating furniture is not something you see every day, and even though she was terrified she couldn't resist peeking out of the bedroom window. (*Our* bedroom, as I'd thought of it till extremely recently.)

To repay her attention, I picked up some of her undies, which I found hanging on Jed's rotary airer, and began draping them on various shrubs and bushes around the garden. OK, it wasn't big and it wasn't clever. Also, I'd scratched my legs on a rosebush and I could feel a broken nail. But it was definitely a problem that had led to an adventure, as my mum might have said.

Through the upstairs window I saw Jane dialling someone. The police? Jed? I pictured my new ex taking the call at his work, trying to stay calm in front of his fellow underwriters. Perhaps he'd be wondering now if he'd chosen the wrong woman? Perhaps he'd be wondering if having a girlfriend who was a nutcase was his punishment for the way he'd strung me along?

Unlikely. He'd probably just be embarrassed by the whole thing. The installation of a free coffee machine was about the most exciting thing that had ever happened in that office, as far as I could tell. I suppose malicious damage from a poltergeist attack might raise some interesting questions in terms of policy coverage, at least?

Anyway, I'd had my fun and with Jane phoning people it was time for a sharp exit. I slipped back out of the gate and padded back to the car which, by fluke rather than foresight, I happened to have parked out of sight of the house. I was in the clear. And I was clear of Jed too, whether or not I wanted to be.

After an uneventful evening, during the whole of which my body stubbornly refused to show itself, I had a couple of drinks and headed for bed. I hadn't exactly done much but somehow, with all the shock and upset of the day, I was exhausted.

As I slid under the duvet for an early night, I felt my phone vibrate.

How you doing? it said simply. *Fancy a drink tomorrow night? x*

Wow, that didn't take long. I picked up the phone and I texted Jed straight back: *I can't see you.*

I snuggled under the welcoming embrace of my covers, and dreamed wonderful dreams of being unmissably, flagrantly, obscenely *visible*.

It was 3.12am when I woke again. I put on my outfit, slipped out to the Corsa, and drove a couple of careful miles.

Outside the old Convent, I parked up and stripped off. I'd always wondered about the security here and sure enough, with an attendant smoking by the open front door, it was easy enough to slip inside. I even had time to rub my hands with a bit of alcoholic gel.

I slipped along one blue-lino-ed corridor after another, and up a red-lino-ed staircase, its steps edged with strips of health-and-safety rubber. A low hum of always-on equipment filled the place. Occasionally, somewhere deep in the building, the bang of an automatic door opening and closing on a crude metal arm battered the calm. Everywhere there was that familiar and dreaded smell, some combination of disinfectant, boiled veg and air freshener, with a faint but unmistakable undernote of piss.

I slipped past the nurse playing Candy Crush behind a desk at the end of mum's corridor, and opened her door.

I could make out her form in the half-light. Her slight frame was bunched over to one side of the bed, pointed diagonally at her bedside table, on which sat a glass of water, a man-size box of tissues and a picture book of the

Impressionists that I'd got for her once. She was snoring gently, almost musically. As she exhaled, her mouth made a light buzzing, hissing sort of sound. I sat quietly in the IKEA chair by her bed, and stroked her lank hair. She started in her sleep. *Parakeet! Parakeetomol!*

She was always one for wordplay.

'Ssssh, mum,' I whispered back, holding her hand once more. 'Sssh. Sleep now. I've got you.' She settled again, nuzzling her forehead into my palm.

My phone vibrated. It was Lynne, texting to say she wouldn't be in today as she'd already been up half the night. *This is a hell of a bug,* she said. *I keep wanting to throw up. Unless . . . ? You don't think?*

Mum rolled over. *Go to bluebells, darling, Pretty blue. Blueblue,* she said to herself, her mouth forming an awkward, hoarse half-smile.

You never know, I texted back.

The back of mum's room looked over a little scrappy park, with a couple of swings in it and a sparse patch of bluebells round an old oak. Mum liked to stare out at this because it reminded her of the fabled bluebell woods of her childhood. Nothing again had ever been so blue, as she'd been reminding me all my life.

'Ssssshhh mum,' I whispered, squeezing her hand. 'I've got you. I see you.'

Next day Zoe and Shania(?) had to be rescued from the roof of Canary Wharf. Cowering with fear and hypothermia, they could not satisfactorily account for their actions and the police were considering charges. Jav was stranded in the Alps somewhere, and Arvi had to be rescued by a lifeboat out of Lowestoft.

And when I woke in my chair, naked but for a tartan blanket, I could see my broken nail, and my mum was at peace.

WHO IS MY NEIGHBOUR ?

Eva Wilch, Castle View Estate
Missing: Kookoo, much-loved tabby cat – can you help??
Hi all, just to say that our 13-year-old tabby cat went missing the night before last. Hasn't been seen since Tuesday 9pm. She's normally a real homebody, rarely leaves the house or garden. She has brown and yellow markings in rough stripes across her back and a white patch on her back left leg. Collar says KOOKOO + our mobile but may have slipped off. We're on the corner of Bodiam Road and Lincoln Drive. Please check your sheds and garages. She's a much-loved family member and we're very worried.
13 Sept – Castle View Estate – Tags: <u>Can you help?</u>

Basil Delpierre, Castle View Estate
Anyone recommend a plumber?
Can anyone recommend a local plumber who is reliable and won't cost an arm and a leg? (Big ask I know!!) I have an issue with the programme settings on my combi boiler, which may or may not be connected to a weird howling noise that keeps emanating from the taps in the night. Well, I think it's the taps – just when I think I've tracked down the source of the noise, it seems to have moved on to another part of the house . . . ?
13 Sept – Castle View Estate – Tags: <u>Trusted tradespeople</u> | <u>Can you help?</u>

Don Hedley, Border Hill
Strip club or kebab shop?
Does anyone know the real purpose of the new "kebab shop" that's opening on Stirling Lane, just to the left of the Old Wetherspoons? At least they *say* it's going to be a kebab place, but the name is Meat On A Stick [sic] and the flyer I've got shows a pic of a scantily clad woman cavorting around a big slab of meat on what looks like some sort of S&M trapeze. (Looks a bit like the Purple Reins Sex Swing from Lovehoney.com, but how would I know). A friend with spies in the planning department tells me they're applying for a licence for a bar upstairs. Is nowhere safe? Wonder if it would be a membership thing and how much men would be charged to indulge their peccadillos? All very tasteless advertising even if the rest is not true.

15 Sept – Border Hill – Tags: <u>Local happenings</u> | <u>Opening and closing</u> | <u>Can you help?</u>

> *Eva Wilch, Castle View Estate*
> This is disgusting. I have two teenage daughters and in the age of #metoo it's incredible that people (i.e. men) can still get away with this filth. Perhaps we could organise a RoundMyWay petition on here?

> *Don Hedley, Border Hill*
> Well said Eva. Best option ahead of formal protest may be to attend the club or whatever incognito, perhaps do some secret filming and try to get a sense of the scale of the perversity involved. Not exactly pleasant, but happy to help out for the good of the community.

> *FatBeats, Border Hill*
> Lol! Thanks for looking out for us Don! So sorry you have to put yourself through this, hope at least you get a decent bit of chilli sauce with your ~~boner~~ doner.

Basil Delpierre, Castle View Estate
Is Alexa sentient?
OK bit of a controversial headline, but I'm wondering whether this voice-activated tech has gone a bit too far?? About 3am this morning, I was violently woken from my slumbers to hear a high-pitched wailing sound. It was like a seagull in pain, or a baby being tortured. I grabbed my glasses, went next door and saw that the blue circle on my Amazon Echo Dot had lit up. The noises seemed to be coming from there. Opinions and thoughts please – especially if you have a background in tech.
16 Sept – Castle View Estate – Tags: Can you help? | Tech talk

> *Eva Wilch, Castle View Estate*
> I agree, automation has gone too far. Last night I was having a (not very serious) discussion with my hubby about the cost of insuring an oil tanker, and this morning my internet searches are full of ads for marine reinsurance software??
> PS Yes – we do have an Alexa, though we've taken to whispering in her vicinity . . .

> *Don Hedley, Border Hill*
> Hi – that's so funny! Had the same thing last week. Was chatting about erectile dysfunction (in a purely academic sense) and next day there were ads for clinics all over my internet!!!

> *FatBeats, Border Hill*
> Basil, did you not just think to unplug it? @Don, sounds like you need a stick for your meat!!!

> *Basil Delpierre, Castle View Estate*
> FatBeats I did! But that was the funny thing. I still heard noises after that, but more sort of muffled. Kind of like a sort of evil cackling and that sort of fiendish whispering sound that gets

18

into the corner of your mind just when you're trying to sleep, and you just know you're going to have that nightmare about the face on the stairs again, you know?

> *Eva Wilch, Castle View Estate*
> You've lost me there, I'm afraid Basil. My nightmares are just the boring ones about losing teeth. What do your family say about all this??

Basil Delpierre, Castle View Estate
Mattress for sale
Double mattress available for collection. Lots of life left in it for the right couple.
16 Sept – Castle View Estate – Tags: Buying and selling | Can you help?

> *FatBeats, Border Hill*
> Wow. Wasn't this a Hemingway short story??

Basil Delpierre, Castle View Estate
Bright lights overhead – any ideas??
I was outside my house about 11pm last night, just fetching some bits from the garage. As I closed up, I heard a beeping sound above me and looked up to see what must have been a drone flying not far overhead. When I looked round I could see 8 or 10 more, all with little red and white lights flashing, all making little whirring and beeping noises. Anyone know what this is? Is it the police? Is it even legal?
18 Sept – Castle View Estate – Tags: Local happenings | Tech talk | Crime and safety | Can you help?

> *Eva Wilch, Castle View Estate*
> Hi Basil, could be the police – we heard several helicopters again in the night, think it may be to do with that drugs bust down on Lewes Avenue last weekend?

> *Don Hedley, Border Hill*
> It could also be a bunch of lads trying out their new early Xmas pressies! (Or ladies I suppose – don't know why I assume blokes??) It seems odd that so many would be hovering over a single house like that. I do hope they weren't trying to spy on you naked or anything like that!! I've accidentally captured a few bits of footage of people sunbathing in gardens with mine!!

> *Paul Pond, Border Hill*
> Don't want to scare the horses, but has it occurred to anyone that this could be thieves trying to find out whether your house is occupied, what your security system is like etc?? Apparently they can hack into your smartmeter and work out what time your lights go off and watch your telly and everything. I've woken up and found my telly on a different channel before. I have a mate in the Freemasons who met a guy from CID at one of their dos the other night, and he says thieves use drones to work out where the police are, so they can plan their night's burglaries without fear of getting nicked. Also the army use them apparently to see if any illegals are living in outbuildings or growing hydroponics in lofts etc . . .

> *FatBeats, Border Hill*
> Dude, the army don't do the drug stuff!!

> *Paul Pond, Border Hill*
> That's not what I've heard. And I've got an uncle in the Sussex Rifles.

> *Peter Fenster, Castle View Estate*
> Like social media and over-reaching EU red tape, drones are a modern-day curse. I don't think you can legally shoot one down, alas. But you can shoot one down illegally quite easily, with a decent air rifle (!). FYI I read the principality of Monaco

apparently hired a company to install a high-tech system to detect, monitor and block drones. This may be a bit beyond our budgets at the present time, but if the nuisance continues I'm sure the price of such things will come down. Perhaps we could crowdfund a defence system for our whole neighbourhood's airspace? (Or at least the Castle View side.)

> *Paul Pond, Border Hill*
Talking to a guy last night who's worked closely with Google, and he says what's happening now is just the tip of the iceberg. They've got new tech that uses algorithms and predictive sentiment analysis to basically work out what we're going to search for . . . before we even know it ourselves! It's all gone way too far but who's going to stop them? Not the politicians, that's for sure, because Google have already got all the dirt on them from data surveillance, listening records, search history tracking etc. We're screwed basically.

> *Eva Wilch, Castle View Estate*
Am guessing you're not a Remainer, @Peter?

> *Paul Pond, Border Hill*
Plus Taylor Swift is using facial recognition on her fans now. She says it's to detect stalkers, but I've heard it's to spot anyone who's not dancing around enough so she can ban them from future concerts.

> *FatBeats, Border Hill*
They'll be sending bots to crawl our dreams next . . .

> *Mary Tomkinson, Castle View Estate*
Hi Basil, I'm in your road – a few doors up I think, and we didn't hear anything at all. You don't think it was your crazy Alexa again do you??!

> *Basil Delpierre, Castle View Estate*
Do you really think so Dr FatBeats? That would explain so much!

> *Peter Fenster, Castle View Estate*
Not sure that it's appropriate to speculate on other people's politics, Eva, and pretty sure RoundMyWay isn't the forum for it. But I'm glad at least that you find something to laugh at in the prospect of a once-great country resigning itself to loss of its sovereignty, its control over its own borders, and its right to trade freely with the whole world.

> *FatBeats, Border Hill*
Dude what u bin smokin!!

Jo Kari, Castle View Estate
Fancy a makeover for party season? Yey!
Hi all – I'm Jo, I'm a qualified holistic beauty therapist and makeup artist with 14 years' experience. I work out of my home beauty studio here in Melbourne Road, and as I've just joined RoundMyWay I wanted to let you all know that I have a few slots left in the run-up to Christmas. So if you fancy a session to get yourself ready for a big night out, or if you want some advice on a good look for the holidays, just give me a shout. Wardrobe consultancy and personal shopping consultations available too. For those of you who'd like to give the gift of beauty this Xmas, giftcards and 'beauty season tickets' are available too.
4 Nov – Castle View Estate – Tags: <u>Trusted tradespeople</u> | <u>Health and wellbeing</u> | <u>Buying and selling</u>

Christine Allerby, Border Hill
Good to be alive!
Hello fellow RoundMyWay-ers! This morning, I woke early, made myself an espresso, and stood outside on my patio in my dressing

gown. The air had a bracing bite to it, a pretty pattern of crisscrossing con trails scored the sky-blue morning sky, birds chattered and buzzed, and next door's water feature tinkled agreeably. And I suddenly thought that, here and now, in among all the doom and gloom about Brexit and Trump and climate change, the world is still an extraordinary place, and it's a blessing to be alive, just to have made it this far, to this day. So whoever you are, reading this, know that you are loved and forgiven. Cherish this very moment. Yes, you! And yes, this day! This moment!

And if you ever fancy a cuppa and a bit of company, you'll always find a warm welcome at our coffee mornings in the church hall at St John the Evangelist, on Richmond Row. Don't worry, no strings or funny talk – we're just a bunch of folk living happily in the light of the Lord, who happen to do a fabulously frothy cappuccino for just £1.20. Hope to see you there one day!
6 Nov – Border Hill – Tags: <u>Local happenings</u> | <u>Health and wellbeing</u>

Basil Delpierre, Castle View Estate
Anyone had rats?
Can anyone suggest a good rodent extermination company? I keep hearing scratching behind my walls and skirting boards. It's worse at night. Lots of noise coming from Mother's room.
9 Nov – Castle View Estate – Tags: <u>Trusted tradespeople</u>

> *Mary Tomkinson, Castle View Estate*
> You need The Rat Lady. Can't find her number to hand, but just google her – she's got a website and she's based somewhere local-ish like Cloud Park. She's never let me down yet!

> *Basil Delpierre, Castle View Estate*
> Thanks! Will try her. It's getting to the point where I can still hear the noise even when I'm not in the house any more. It's almost as if the rats were in my mind. Or maybe i

Mary Tomkinson, Castle View Estate
Can you mend my Pane??
Hi all, looking to get a cracked panel fixed in my infinity balustrade. Sorry to post about this a third time but original manufacturer has now gone into receivership and says they can't legally recommend anyone else. Surely someone can replace? Have included picture this time.
12 Nov – Castle View Estate – Tags: <u>Trusted tradespeople</u> | <u>Can you help?</u>

> *FatBeats, Border Hill*
> 'Infinity balustrade'??!! – I think if you'd just said in the first place that you needed a new pane of glass for your little balcony wall, then people might have had a vague scooby what you were going on about!

> *Peter Fenster, Castle View Estate*
> Ignore him! Double Bubble the glaziers should be able to help, Mary. They're not the cheapest but they're very versatile and take on all sorts of jobs. At least they'll be able to tell you if it's possible. Their work is always very sensitive to local fabric too. Have messaged you their details.

Mary Tomkinson, Castle View Estate
Please take my broken white goods away!
I have a broken extractor hood with motor intact, a dishwasher with a door that won't seal, and a fridge-freezer with worn lining. All are yours for the taking if you can carry them away!
12 Nov – Castle View Estate – Tags: <u>Can you help?</u>

> *FatBeats, Border Hill*
> Wow, you're really selling them to us, Mary! Just leave them out the front like everyone else, and the men in white vans will come and take them.

> *Peter Fenster, Castle View Estate*
> I haven't been through your way as yet today, Mary, but I do hope these items are not cluttering up the pavement? Contrary to the comment above, it is NOT advisable to leave things out for 'men in white vans' to pick up. They are unauthorised operatives who follow no health & safety guidelines and, once encouraged, will no doubt start ferreting around in bins, driveways and other people's front gardens given half a chance. Please make use of the proper channels – that's what our community charge is for!!

> *FatBeats, Border Hill*
> One word, bro. Chillax.

> *Peter Fenster, Castle View Estate*
> 'Chillax' is not a word.

> *FatBeats, Border Hill*
> Actually, bro, it is.

> *Peter Fenster, Castle View Estate*
> I think I probably know more about what constitutes a word than someone who calls themselves FatBeats and can probably only really express themselves via the medium of emoticons.

> *FatBeats, Border Hill*
> Actually, bro, for your information I'm a postgrad researcher currently completing an MPhil in pragmatic philology at Birkbeck, so I have science on my side when I tell you that if you recognise a brief sequence of letters or sounds, and you have a pretty good idea of their communicative intent and context, then chances are you have a real word on your hands. Simply put, wordhood is constituted from the evolving consensus of a community of shared language users, not from

some spurious appeal to etymology or some self-appointed cultural authority. To quote the excellent Johnson blog over at *The Economist*: 'When people criticise non-words, it's usually just a lazy way to criticise their users.'

Peter Fenster, Castle View Estate
3 more car break-ins in one weekend!!!
Having discovered that my car was broken into and the sat nav stolen on Friday night, I'm appalled to report that I have since heard of three separate incidents in which cars have been broken into, or thefts attempted in the past 48 hours. Almost certainly Pikeys coming over from the fairground on Brookmans Common. Police utterly hopeless as usual.
12 Nov – Castle View Estate – Tags: Local happenings | Crime and safety

> *FatBeats, Border Hill*
> Dude, not cool

> *Eva Wilch, Castle View Estate*
> Very sorry to hear your news, Peter. But to expand on what I take to be FatBeats' point, could I ask that you refrain from using the word 'Pikey'?? It's generally considered to be quite offensive and, in all fairness, we don't know who the perpetrators of any of these incidents were – or, indeed, if they were all connected.

Mary Tomkinson, Castle View Estate
PVC or aluminium?
Does anyone know of an affordable supplier of bay windows? The original French-style wooden frames we have are very elegant but not very exactly draught-proof. Thinking about PVC or aluminium replacements but obviously concerned about the look. Has anyone done this recently? Could you recommend someone?
12 Nov – Castle View Estate – Tags: Can you help? | Trusted tradespeople

> *Peter Fenster, Castle View Estate*
PLEASE. DO. NOT. FIT. PVC!!! Insensitive window installations have already been a massive plight on the whole aesthetic heritage and character of this whole estate. Please do not add to the problem!!!

> *FatBeats, Border Hill*
Tempted to suggest PVC just to annoy Peter F, as he's clearly so obsessed about it. But actually they do look a bit icky. Btw, @Peter, did you mean 'blight'? I'm sure 'plight' is a word too though.

> *Basil Delpierre, Castle View Estate*
Can anyone recommend windows that stop people seeing in? (Or out?)

> *FatBeats, Border Hill*
Omg, are you the bloke who walks round checking that people's building works conform to your idea of what's in keeping with the character of the neighbourhood? The self-appointed clipboard man? There's a word for people like you.

> *Peter Fenster, Castle View Estate*
I think 'A Good Neighbour' is the phrase you're looking for.

> *Christine Allerby, Border Hill*
Interesting thread – makes me think of that New Testament quote, 'And who is my neighbour?' (Luke 10:29). A lot of people think that Jesus spoke these words, but in fact this was a question that was put to Jesus by 'an expert in the law' (Luke 10:25), in order to test Him out. Jesus' reply, of course, was the Parable of the Good Samaritan, a perfect response that is as eloquent and resonant today as ever it was – especially here on RoundMyWay!

> *FatBeats, Border Hill*
> Holy trolls Batman!

> *FatBeats, Border Hill*
> @Peter that wasn't the phrase I was thinking of. It's slipped my mind for the moment but if it comes back to me I'll let you know when I see you next Tuesday.

> *Peter Fenster, Castle View Estate*
> What is happening next Tuesday? Is there a neighbourhood committee meeting? I wasn't informed.

> *FatBeats, Border Hill*
> <This post has been blocked for inappropriate content>

Basil Delpierre, Castle View Estate
Can anyone recommend an exorcist?
MEND mY PAiiNn??
14 Nov – Castle View Estate – Tags: Trusted tradespeople

> *Jo Kari, Castle View Estate*
> Hi Basil, as well as practising holistic beauty therapy, I am also a chartered spiritual healer, affiliated with the International Council of Mind:Body:Spirit Healers. We don't believe in exorcism as such, as we understand demons and other unwanted spirits to be blockages in your aetheric aura caused by unresolved thoughts and feelings from previous lives, but I'm sure I could help.
>
> I'd suggest an initial aura-cleansing massage, followed by a programme of deep-tissue past-life bodywork. Sounds like it might be easier if I came to you? The initial consultation session is free, and I can talk you through the rates after that. It's obviously very specialised work, and insurance won't touch

28

this I'm afraid, but the benefits in terms of psychic resolution and whole-soul liberation will leave you so much richer in other ways. Just pop me a DM, darling, and we can make a start!

> *Mary Tomkinson, Castle View Estate*
Can't recommend Jo highly enough! She helped me out with both of my pregnancies, and as well as soothing aching muscles and dispelling anxiety, I learnt some valuable life lessons and philosophies that have stood me in good stead in all sorts of areas of my life. A truly healing and empowering experience! (Jo – just paste in and edit if too gushing/not gushing enough.)

> *Don Hedley, Border Hill*
Very intrigued by the bodywork angle Jo! Are there any videos or demos I could take a look at? Would be good to apply some of that deep-tissue work on my blockage.

> *Christine Allerby, Border Hill*
Let me tell you a story. 'When Jesus arrived on the other side in the region of the Gadarenes, He was met by two demon-possessed men coming from the tombs. They were so violent that no one could pass that way . . . In the distance a large herd of pigs was feeding. The demons begged Jesus, "If You drive us out, send us into the herd of pigs." "Go!!" He told them. So they came out and went into the pigs, and the whole herd rushed down the steep bank into the sea and perished in the waters . . .'

Powerful stuff, no? Many people are surprised to learn that the Church of England – with which, as Pentecostal Evangelicals, we are fully allied – does still practise exorcism today. And you'll be delighted that our very own Reverend Tony Simming was recently designated Minister of Deliverance for our diocese (by the Bishop himself no less!) I've shared your details with Tony, and he is praying on your situation, awaiting the discernment of the Lord as to the best next step. However, to make sure that this is indeed a genuine case of possession (and not, say, epilepsy or homosexual panic, as can happen), he asks if you have experienced at least 3 of the following:

- Strange visions, for instance of unexplained lights or voices in your head
- A feeling that others can read your mind, or that you can read theirs
- A feeling of rage or deep anxiety when you pass a church
- A sudden reluctance to cook with salt (Satan hates salt)
- An urge to watch horror movies or listen to thrash metal
- Seeking knowledge through bogus spiritual practices such as astrology, osteopathy or Indian head massage
- An obsession with Love Island, sexual promiscuity or Asian food
- An urge to hurt animals, especially livestock

In the meantime, stay calm, keep praying, and have the Bible always with you. If you fancy dropping in for a coffee at St John's one morning this week, we can let you have a vial of holy water too – something else Satan hates!

Basil Delpierre, Castle View Estate
So sorry
I am most heartbroken to report that I ran over a cat this morning. The cat, which is a sort of tabby colour with a white foot, seemed quite elderly and manky and confused, and backed out into the road unseen from behind the tyre of a parked car. I had no warning at all, there was no time to do anything. I'm so sorry. I have the remains – if

this is your animal, please contact me privately through the site and accept my most heartfelt condolences.

15 Nov – Castle View Estate – Tags: Can you help? | Local happenings

> *Mary Tomkinson, Castle View Estate*
> Oh this is so sad all round. It sounds like my neighbour Eva's cat. I will go round and see her if she hasn't heard the news. And it must have been very traumatic for you too Basil – it sounds like you couldn't have done anything about it.

Eva Wilch, Castle View Estate
Mail received in error
Through my door this morning I've received a bundle of letters addressed to a Ms Veronique Werter. The letters are airmailed and seem quite old; no one to my knowledge has ever lived here of that name (and we've been here since the mid-nineties!). Can anyone shed any light on this mystery?

16 Nov – Castle View Estate – Tags: Can you help?

> *Mary Tomkinson, Castle View Estate*
> Ooh Eva! Perhaps you should open them and see what they say – could be inspiration for another of your wonderful cozy mysteries! (How is the writing going by the way??)

> *Basil Delpierre, Castle View Estate*
> Torment me not, Eva Wilch = Evil Witch! You know full well that Veronique Werter was my mother's maiden name. Those letters were to her gnostic priest and confessor, Monsignor Lafayette, and have not left the room in which she died since I locked it 17 years ago. Those letters contain the secrets of her work with the White Knights of Avalon, and were not to be read by anyone, not even her son, except in extremis. Yesterday, with the demons closing in, I did break the seal of her chamber at last, to seek out their wisdom . . . only to find

her drawer broken into and the contents missing!! Oh how I could have done with their wisdom in this, my hour of darkest need! Again and again I bid you leave me, Evil Witch, but still I hear your voice in my Dyson!! Oh chillax, my infinite balustrade!

> *FatBeats, Border Hill*
Dude, the White Knights of Avalon . . . Were they like a prog rock outfit?? Or is this more like the KKK??

> *Mary Tomkinson, Castle View Estate*
There's a guy on Lancaster Way who's an absolute genius with broken hoovers. Tiny little place, easy to miss. He's been there years.

> *Eva Wilch, Castle View Estate*
Basil, I have to confess that I haven't the faintest clue what you're talking about! But I'm glad to find a home for these letters, which I have of course left unopened. If you can DM me your address I'll pop them round this afternoon. Is yours by any chance the house with the giant statue of the Virgin in the front garden, next to that six foot quartz grotto thing that sits in a cloud of incense under all those wind chimes??

> *Peter Fenster, Castle View Estate*
Basil, is that your place? I noticed your new additions to the frontal area on one of my recent rounds, and I did wonder if we might have a word? I'm all for freedom of religious expression (up to a point) but I do think you have to respect the local cultural and aesthetic norms, which are very well established and have been built up over several decades. And to be frank, the red crosses sprayed over all your doors and windows are an especial eyesore.

Jo Kari, Castle View Estate
Mindful hypno-zen birthing
Hi all, back by popular demand . . . my courses for expectant mums (and dads) start again in January. If you're anxious about the birth, or just fancy a bit of soothing me-time, I'll be covering: transformational foetal massage, pre-partum confidence building, empowered embryo visualisations and – for single mums – the ever-popular Dad Detox! First session free when you sign up for six or more. See my website for full details.
19 Nov – Castle View Estate – Tags: <u>Health & wellbeing</u>

> *Don Hedley, Border Hill*
> Sounds like a very interesting range, Jo! Can single dads attend?? (Only joking) If I had a good lady wife, of course, I'm sure we would be working hard, as it were, to get to a point where she would be in a position to avail herself of your holistic ministrations. (wink wink!)

> *Basil Delpierre, Castle View Estate*
> Nay lady succubus! The demons whinny at my gate, but they shall not impregnate me! Never will they violate me with their seed! I shall not bring forth the evil French-style child! My womb is sealed with finest Pikey aluminium!

Eva Wilch, Castle View Estate
You mad cat murderer
Basil, you heartless batshit-crazy fucked-up cat killer! I've just realised it was you who murdered Kookoo. And how dare you suggest she was manky and not with it!! She was a fine-looking animal and perfectly alert last time we saw her!! As co-admin of this forum, I must inform you that your membership status is now under review.
20 Nov – Castle View Estate – Tags: <u>Crime and safety</u> | <u>Health & wellbeing</u> | <u>Local happenings</u>

> *Basil Delpierre, Castle View Estate*
> In my defence, I was ordered to make a sacrifice, and an ageing animal like this, that was already suffering from memory loss, probably made for a much less controversial target than other options, animal and human, that I considered. The voices were very clear; hopefully they will vacate my mindspace now. Perhaps they will move on to yours. In which case, God help you.

Mary Tomkinson, Castle View Estate
Pair of glasses found on Stepney Street
A pair of specs were sitting on top of a post box in Stepney Street, as I went past yesterday morning (Tuesday). Tortoiseshell frames, probably a man's? Perhaps dropped out of someone's pocket as they were leaning over to post something?? As they were still there when I returned a couple of hours later, I have taken them with me for safekeeping. DM me via the site if they're yours.
21 Nov – Castle View Estate – Tags: Can you help?

> *Basil Delpierre, Castle View Estate*
> Mine eyes! Mine eyes! Cover mine eyes in deep-tissue PVC!! Consult my wardrobe! Extract my hood! Unblock my previous lives! But . . . meet not the gaze of the giant Torture Tortoise!!

> *FatBeats, Border Hill*
> Dude, you sound like a bot!

Basil Delpierre, Castle View Estate
A sign at last!!
After the storms last night, I awoke to find a large visitant on my lawn. A giant aquamarine scallop shell, clearly a sign from Saint James of Compostela that God has heard my prayers and his saints are working to intercede on my behalf. Praise be! (Image attached)

Do you know the story? *James, the brother of Jesus, was persecuted and killed in the Holy Land for preaching about his brother. After he died his remains found their way to Galicia, in northern Spain. As the ship carrying James got close to the shore, legend has it that a horse with a young man on his back panicked and rode headlong into the sea. But by a miracle, man and horse were saved, and emerged from the waves covered in scallop shells – still to this day, the sacred symbol of all pilgrims who walk the way of St James to his shrine at Santiago de Compostela.*

Having ridden on the back of a crazed demon, and feared for my life in the swelling waters of madness and possession, now I too emerge at last onto the scallop-strewn shores of health and holiness. Hallelujah!

27 Nov – Castle View Estate – Tags: Health & wellbeing

> *FatBeats, Border Hill*
> Hate to crash your vibe, dude, but that pic you've got there is one of those little plastic pond liners.

ACTIVE AND PASSIVE VOICE

In English we can distinguish between two voices: **active and passive.**

Voice is useful for helping to choose **which part of a sentence we want to focus on**. And contrary to some popular advice, using the passive voice doesn't automatically make you a passive person!

Telling active and passive apart
The difference between active and passive is easier to show than to explain, so let's start with some examples:
    [1] Jane did all the washing for them both.

This is an active sentence. The subject *Jane* of the verb *washed* is also the one doing the action. This **coincidence of subject of verb and doer of action** is key to identifying and understanding the active voice.

Now you might think the subject of the verb in a sentence is always the doer of the action. Not so! Take this example:
    [2] The washing was done by Jane (every single week).

Here the subject is *the washing,* and the verb phrase it goes with is *was done.* But, contrary to what some (ie Jim) might think, the clothes didn't just wash themselves. *Jane* did the washing, again, but though the sentence is describing the same state of affairs as example [1], she is no longer the subject of the verb, but has been relegated to a position at the end of the sentence.

The doer of the verb in a passive sentence is known as **the agent**. The agent is easy to spot because they are usually **preceded by** *with* **or** *by*. For example:

[3] She'd often been told *by her mates* what a loser he was.

So [2] and [3] are examples of a passive sentence, where the recipient of the action, rather than the doer of the action, becomes the grammatical subject. This is a very useful construction when we want to put the focus of our sentence on the person or thing on the receiving end of the action. For example:

[4] *Her head had been turned* by his roguish good looks, his way with a guitar, and the fact that he was the only bloke she'd ever met who would get up and dance. For a while, this actually seemed enough.

[5] *She was easily persuaded* to let him move in when he lost his flat. It would only be for a few weeks, he said.

[6] It wasn't just the washing. Day after day, *carpets were hoovered, food was bought, dinners were cooked, the dish-washer was emptied,* and *the toilet bowl was scrubbed* – while Jim sat sucking on his bong staring at Ariana Grande videos claiming to be seeking 'inspiration for my break-through album'.

[7] *Her pleas for a more equal arrangement about house stuff were met* with sulky indifference, sardonic eye-rolls, and

protestations that, like, 'I can't right now, babe, I'm in the flow'.

We might call example [7] an instance of the passive-aggressive voice. This is not strictly a grammatical category, of course, though the behaviour was very real and endlessly repeated.

Formation of the passive

The classic passive construction consists of a **conjugated form of the verb *be* + a past tense participle**. For example:

[8] When her mum *was + knocked* down by a van and her leg *was + broken* in two places, Jim couldn't even be arsed to go and see her in the hospital (even though she'd lent him all that cash for studio time so he could put his demo together).

[9] He *was + given* so many chances to sort his shit out.

[10] She *was + filled* with a sudden rage at the thought of how much time she'd wasted on him.

If the doer is known as the agent, the recipient of the action is known as the **patient**. And by God, she had been.

The short passive

In the following examples, we've put the agent in square brackets. Try reading them with and without the agent.

[11] I've had a shit day at work and I'd just like a cup of tea, thought Jane. But the milk's all been used up again [by Jim].

[12] Why was she expected [by Jim] to be the bread-winner and the skivvy in their relationship, while he just sat up smoking and 'jamming' all night and slept through the day?

[13] What about her goals and ambitions? Why weren't they ever taken seriously [by Jim]?

[14] She noticed his teeth had been whitened [by an expensive cosmetic dentist, no doubt], and wondered where'd he got the money.

As you'll have noticed, it's perfectly possible in these examples to dispense with the agent altogether and for the sentence to still make perfect sense. This construction is known as a **short passive**.

There are lots of reasons why we might want to dispense with the agent. Perhaps it's just obvious:

[15] Her hot flushes, night sweats and moodiness were not remarked upon, apart from in the odd reference to 'shark week' or 'riding the cotton pony'. She didn't tell him she wasn't actually having periods any more.

Perhaps the agent isn't central to the story we want the sentence to tell:

[16] *He'd been seen* flirting with the girl behind the bar at The Roxy.

[17] *All his gigs had been cancelled*, she found out, though it wasn't clear if there'd really been any in the first place.

Or perhaps we're not sure who the agent is:

[18] 'Do you not *feel loved*, babe?' he'd always ask, shooting her his special look, whenever they had an argument. 'Don't you know how much *you're adored?*' 'Who by?' she answered flatly.

Myths about the passive
The passive is not a tense. Indeed, passive sentences can be constructed with any tense or aspect. For example:

[19] *Cash was withdrawn* from the shared account again yesterday – the one they were supposed to use only for rent and emergencies.

[20] *More of her cash is probably being withdrawn right now,* as he's just gone out to the pub again with his druggie muso mates, and he hasn't earned anything for months.

[21] *More money will no doubt be taken out tomorrow,* unless she does something.

Using the passive isn't always a sign of bad writing. It's very useful in certain contexts. As well as enabling us to switch the focus of a sentence onto the element we want to prioritise, it also allows us to put to the end of the sentence any element we have a lot to say about. For example:

[22] She was accompanied to the specialist by her sister, *who was the one person who'd never tried to judge their relationship but who was obviously secretly delighted that Jane was finally thinking of kicking this deadbeat out of her life once and for all.*

Using the passive doesn't automatically make you a shirker of responsibility. Because of the agent-less short passive, people think the passive is a weasely part of speech used by people trying to evade responsibility for things. In fact, this effect is just as possible in the active voice. For example:

[23] 'Plans are for squares, babe,' he always said, in those rare moments when she dared to ask about how things stood between them. 'That's not how we roll.'

[24] 'Let's not rush things,' he said. 'If a baby wants us, it'll come knocking.'

Using the passive voice doesn't have to mean you're passive! People commonly confuse the passive voice with passivity as a character flaw. Certainly it's true that, historically, the passive has been used to reinforce stereotypical gender roles. A woman for many centuries could not *marry*, she could only *be married*, for example; and certain verbs of sexual intercourse followed a similar pattern until relatively recently in our cultural history.

But sometimes the passive construction can signal a proactive decision, however difficult. For example:

[25] The cause of premature ovarian failure is often unknown.

[26] By the time he woke up next day, the locks had been changed and most of his stuff had been piled neatly in bin bags in the hall.

[27] The sabotage of his vintage Fender – the one thing he really cared about, apart from himself – wouldn't be spotted for several hours at least.

Final exercise

Look at the following sentences and decide which clauses are in the active or the passive voice:

[28] Friends' calls and texts were not answered; Jane wanted to be left alone with her sadness.

[29] Dimly she saw a new path ahead, and she knew this sunken feeling was the unavoidable start of it.

[30] She hadn't known how much she wanted a child – till she knew she couldn't have one.

NOW AND FOR EVER

'I am dying,' said the guru and they all thought it was marvellous. Everything he said was marvellous.

'He means that we are all called to *die to ourselves*,' said one. 'That is the way of all spiritual paths, after all.'

'Yes! In dying to the one, we are *born to the many*,' said another. 'Or is it the other way round?'

'It means that he is on the verge of *leaving the ego behind for good*. That he is closing in on *a new level of onehood*.'

'Wow!' said another. 'I feel something already.'

'What I think Master means,' said the one who had known him the longest, the one who had known him when he was just Dave, 'Is that he is physically dying. As in: *about to die*.'

The others laughed. 'You are in on this with him!' said one. 'It is more of his divine mischief, another of the Master's playful tests! But fear not: we will not fail him. We will unravel the truth.'

'Yes!' put in another follower. 'While always being mindful that truth and falsehood are false opposites, as our beloved teacher has always said.'

'Not in this case, I fear,' said his oldest and most realistic friend. 'The scan is just a common-or-garden fact, I'm afraid. And the fact is that Master has about four weeks.'

'Oh you and your holy games!' said another apostle delightedly. 'We will get to the bottom of this!'

The guru lay on a divan in his day room. He was tired suddenly of the relentlessly Oriental theme of his world, of all the rugs and throws and the incense and the sandals. In recent days he had developed a hankering for the things of his first home. This was an alarming development in itself, since his first home had been Gravesend.

Grave's End. Grave. Send. *Dear Lord.* (Not him, the other Lord.) The guru had taught people to read signs in the universe, to discern cosmic intention in every snatch of song, every passing butterfly, every chance encounter. But did he really deserve something as corny as Grave Send?

His inner staff did their best to keep followers at bay, but everyone knew that something exciting was happening, and they were terrified of missing out on a revelation.

The guru was terrified too. He did not want to die.

This man, who had been on *Oprah* and advised Presidents and held stadiums spellbound as he worked live transform-ations on wounded people that were so miraculous he even believed them himself, now sat facing the banality of his own end.

And what he found disturbed him.

This man, with his millions in book sales and his global following and his very own spiritual community, three hundred acres out here in the beautiful wilds of Nebraska, found that he was not to be spared the pain or indignity faced by ordinary mortals. Or the sheer fucking terror.

The guru was fond of propounding alternative remedies and complementary therapies of one kind and another. Indeed, he had even given his name to a few discreet lines of healing amulets and karmic bracelets down the years. But when it came to his own personal health, he discovered that he was strictly a private-clinic-in-Switzerland kind of a guy. This was no time for pissing about.

His followers had readily swallowed the explanations offered by the inner team to account for the guru's many recent absences. He was on retreat. He was moving into an exciting new phase in the development of the Work and would return soon to share the light of his discoveries with all. He was deep in preparation for a new book of spiritual exercises. He was even contemplating the addition of a new chapter to his definitive *Book of the Work*, a chapter with bold and exciting implications for all humanity.

While his community buzzed with the excitement of potential new discoveries, he and his inner ones flew in and out of hospitals and clinics and specialist centres in Europe and North America. He consulted clinical oncologists and royal physicians and maverick professors, and when he didn't hear what he wanted he sought out second and third and fourth opinions. Did they not know who he was? he said. People *needed* him.

Oh we know, said the experts, discreetly supplying their account details to his team. It's just that the carcinoma doesn't.

On his arrival back in Nebraska, the guru could not avoid the usual cavalcade. It seemed that every inhabitant of the town – this town he had designed himself, in accordance with strict anthroposophical principles channelled to him via a mountain-top fasting vision (well, sort of) – had come out to welcome him. They always did.

He was aware of dangerous and embarrassing precedents. But he had no Rolls Royce to drive him 100 yards, no armed militia, no conspicuous indulgences. Instead he drove through the high street in a humble Hyundai. The whole car was bullet-proof and bomb-proof, mind, styled after the Popemobile, and about a hundred security personnel mingled with the crowds along the route.

Namaste, one and all, he said silently to the cheering, swooning throng. *My soul honours your soul.*

After that, he took to his room, and was not seen for days. He sent girlfriends away, saw only a handful of trusted advisers. But even in their eyes, he could sense that they were looking beyond him, with a mixture of fear and excitement and greed. In the room next to his, lawyers and wealth managers hovered.

He even tried healing himself. The ironies! For a man who had achieved international fame as a fearless healer of all ills, physical, emotional and spiritual, he was alarmed to discover how little he knew about the body. He spent hours googling cancer.

His enemy, he read, was a group of abnormal cells that could divide without control and even spread to other parts of the body *if they so chose*. Ah of course! He would make them choose otherwise. He would meditate and visualise and pray until they went away. He would turn them on themselves until they conspired to make him well again. Not just well, in fact; he would turn them into mutant anti-cancer cells with the power to imbue his organism with quantum, optimum health! To make him the best he could ever be!

What a legacy, what a legend: the man who made cancer his bitch!

It was a long time since he had actually sat down and done any of this intense praying and chanting stuff. And he was tired. Every day, he was more tired than the day before. He could feel the energy seeping from him with the slightest effort, like flour through a sieve, and with it his will to fight back.

Rage against the dying of the light? Embrace the Great Teacher of Our Impermanence? Soar into the holy oneness?

He found he'd rather watch telly.

Out in the community, the rumours about the Master's silences and non-appearances swirled and escalated.

'Master is communicating with the ascended ones.'

'He has achieved such a level of enlightenment that it is hard for him to return to Body. The liberated spirit lives in a realm of pure joy; to return to the limitations of the physical is exquisitely painful.'

'Our dearly beloved has discovered the secret of infinity. Now he seeks only a way to share it with us.'

'He travels further than any seeker before him. We should be very proud.'

'Yes! But . . . I know it is a selfish thing to say, but I miss his talks.'

'Yes! And his smile.'

'His jokes!'

'Yes! His crazy dry English sense of humour!'

No one seriously believed that Master could die, of course, but they feared that his studies might take him to a place where he would have to leave his people behind.

This was a worrying thought, because the Master was their Light. They had left their old selves behind them when they came out here, from Darjeeling and Dijon and Darwin. It had been like shedding an old unwanted skin, and without Him they did not quite know who they would be any more.

They knew that the Master was for the world, of course, for all men and women, present and future (and past too, somehow). But when you had given up so much for him, however willingly, it was hard not to feel a little proprietorial.

*

'David,' his mother said to him in a dream. 'You must try and eat. Keep up your strength.'

It was a measure of how sick he was that he was actually seeing visions again, such as – whisper it – he had not experienced for decades. Here, incredibly, his mother stood in the room before him. He saw her frown of concern, heard that crisp unflinching voice, felt her hand-creamed palm apply itself appraisingly to his forehead, smelled the inevitable lavender.

'David,' said his only friend. 'Your mum is here.'

He would have sat bolt upright if he could. He had not seen her for seven years, since the last falling-out.

The path he had chosen had never sat well with his mum. A low-key Quaker, she couldn't see beyond the razzmatazz, the crowds, the TV appearances to the really important stuff that he'd been doing: helping people to reconnect with each other – with their souls, which was ultimately the same thing – at a time when the world was threatening to destroy itself. What was it that journalist had said? 'At a time of dangerous division, Deva has made brotherly and sisterly love credible again. He wants nothing more than for people to look each other in the eye once more.'

OK it was a journalist for their own magazine, *Oneness*, but still it was beautifully and simply put. He had only wanted to help people. But in his mum's eyes, he had given in to the lure of showbiz and narcissistic hysteria and basically become a cult leader.

He always remembered her parting words to him after their last argument: 'You should never have given up the clarinet!' Perhaps she was right. He could have taken that scholarship. He'd have been quite a decent chamber musician.

A curtain of weariness and pain cleared briefly from his eyes, and he saw his mother now, as if for the first time. She was older than he remembered. Her eyes were sad and her face drawn. She was trying hard, he knew, to smile at him in a way that for the time being expressed no disapproval.

'Jesus,' he said out loud. 'I'm iller than I thought.'

There is no death. Death is only the return to the whole. To the joy of the One.

When I come to 'die', I will ask my friends to dress me in a simple robe and to prepare an open wooden bier for me. Let them carry me to an open space, let those who care to join us sing and dance and cheer. A grand fiesta of 'finality'!

Then, when the time is come, as the last glimmers are draining from my mortal casing, let them take a torch and light my bier. Let everyone look into my eyes and see me smiling and laughing and singing in the face of this terrible enemy we call 'death'!

Let them see that Death is the beginning, not the end. Let them watch me soar joyfully into the One!!

May I burn slow and true! Let them see me lick the flames that lick my corpse!

Listless, he let the book fall to the floor. It fell open, with the cover still visible – *Meditations on Mortality*, his first bestseller.

An assistant, arriving with a tray of food, picked up the book and quickly saw what he had been reading: the controversial if much-quoted 'Fire Sermon'!

'Oh master,' said the assistant, through tears of sorrow and excitement. 'Do you think of this still for when the time comes?'

Brother Deva rolled over and looked at the man square in the face. He was young and keen and strong, his own small universe of unique specific potential. The guru felt a sudden pang for all that this other man might have been, had he not been sucked into his orbit. A clarinettist perhaps?

Wires draped and machines beeped. It was an effort to speak now.

'When I come to die,' said the great guru of immortal becoming at last, 'I want to be . . . *completely off my tits.*'

'The better to seize the moment of the walls of separation collapsing, Master?'

'The better not to feel a fucking thing.'

They buried him on a hill overlooking the ranch. He had died in the night, in terrible pain until morphine, at last, tipped him over the edge.

The burning ceremony took place the next day. No one was quite sure what else Brother Deva had ingested in recent days, so for obvious reasons the team were keen for the body to be quickly disposed of. Project Legacy – a secret plan that had been in preparation for several months between the oldest friend and a few elite advisers – kicked in at once.

It was the oldest friend, of course, who stood on the hilltop and gave the eulogy. For most in the outside world, this was their first knowledge of the passing of the celebrated spiritual leader. Behind him, white and grey smoke rose still from a discreetly shaded pyre.

The friend, the one who had known him as Dave, spoke of the incredible privilege of being a witness to the Master's passing. All who had been present felt they would be forever transformed by the experience, he said. And that was not all, as how could it be?

The whole community was vibrating with a tremendous vital energy just now, he said. Several people in the community had reported spontaneous healings very close to the moment of the beloved one's passing, at 03.47 Central Daylight Time. There had even been a birth at exactly the same moment.

'Brother Deva's departure is just another of his celebrated jokes,' his old friend's words rang out to cheers and shouts.

'He moves among us still: with us, in us, beyond us, before us and after us!'

At this point the community cameras zoomed in, and someone handed the guru's oldest friend a tiny bundle of blanket. He smiled and cooed at the little bundle, then pulled back an edge of cotton so that the world could see the face of a newborn baby.

The oldest friend held up the bundle to the sky, in a gesture that chat-show wags would soon be comparing with a certain scene in *The Lion King*.

'Behold our past and our future! Blessed be Brother Deva!'

A baby crying. The community flag rippling in the breeze. A billow of smoke. The cheers were still ringing out as the camera zoomed out and the screen faded, until there was nothing left for anyone to look at but a URL for further information.

IN HERE

You start off being better than expected. A bit too good to be true.

You meet by chance in a pub, where she is talking with a mental-health nurse friend about her work, caring for people with dementia. She is used to people being dismissive of the elderly, but you tell her the story of your struggles with your own grandma, careful to agonise about not having done enough. ('But it sounds like you couldn't have done any more,' she says. 'You mustn't punish yourself. Carers always do this! I've seen it so many times!')

When it turns out you have heard of 'validation therapy', a special interest of hers, it's as if the whole pub can hear the sound of a box being ticked. It's all embarrassingly easy, somehow. Or is this just what right feels like?

On the first date, you are compassionate, courageous, candid. Also endearingly eccentric.

You get each of you to write down your Top 3 Vegetables. When you turn over your serviettes, it turns out you have both got the same three (albeit in a slightly different order: you have (1) courgettes, (2) carrots, (3) broccoli; she has carrots first). It's a story you'll retell many times.

Later that first night, you intervene on behalf of a harassed waitress when a group of boozed-up lads in football gear start to get a bit lairy. There are four of them and one of you. But they are men, alive to violence and its omens. There is an edge in your voice that they hear and she doesn't, and they leave you alone.

What it looks like to her, though, is chivalry of a sort that's rarely seen any more. And reviewing this scene through her eyes, even you feel a touch in awe of yourself.

You go large on the gifts.
She mentions a writer she likes; you go out and buy her his entire back catalogue. (Actually it turns out it was only the one title she liked, rather than the author; the books end up back on sale on Amazon, you note later, slightly second-hand now.)

She loves to watch that *Choir* show, and you spend fruit-less hours emailing and calling the show's office to see if Gareth will come and do an impromptu sing-song for the dementia ward. It doesn't work out. You keep going back to them, but somehow the more you insist, the less they want to know.

You learn to love arthouse. More gifts.
Much of your early relationship revolves around a local arthouse cinema she loves. It comes with an offbeat, whole-food café; it organises talks for members by avant-garde directors; and it runs one of those regular morning showings for mums, where women can breast-feed to mad moody films with titles like *Baise-moi* and *120 days of Sodom*.

You come across a limited-edition print of the cinema painted by a local artist. You buy it for a few hundred quid – quite a statement for a fifth date. She is shocked at your boldness. Destiny beckons.

Suddenly, you know all about Buñuel and Truffaut and Kurosawa, you whose favourite film is secretly *Lord of the Rings: Return of the King*. (She must never know, you decide, about your Dungeons and Dragons past.) And you can't help enjoying a little moment of triumph when you have to point out to one of her girlfriends that Renoir is a filmmaker, not *a painter*!

In bed, you try very hard to please her.
You are energetic, ingenious, imaginative. But later, much later, you wonder whether you put too much pressure on her to have the perfect experience every time. It's been suggested that maybe your experimental efforts felt too much like a tick list you were working through. And that maybe you should have listened more when she said she just wanted a cuddle.

Even at work, you are there for her.
She texts you to say her face has come up in a sudden, unsightly rash. You walk out of your office immediately and go to her.

When your boss (a man) questions you next day about hanging up on a client call without explanation, you cough discreetly, look him straight in the eye, and utter the single word, 'dysmenorrhea'. No more is said on the matter. She loves you for this.

You hurry into another room whenever you feel the need to break wind.
One time, you actually defecate on a sheet of newspaper in the kitchen downstairs, because the toilet's right by the bedroom and you don't want her to have to hear or smell that stuff. Bodily things embarrass you. You don't like to see evidence of her shaving, and she soon learns never to leave her blue packets lying about.

You try with her friends, you really do.
When you meet her best friend, you get really drunk – actually, you turn up really drunk – and find yourself screaming in her face: 'I WANT YOU TO LIKE ME BEST OF ALL!' The best friend gets it's meant to be funny – it's a sort of joke staking of your territory – without seeming to laugh all that much.

(A bit like when, later on that night, you take to lying on the dotted line in the middle of the road, for reasons that are unclear even to you.)

Out and about, you see something unexpected.
You spot her in town, on a day you'd not planned to meet, with someone you don't know. You feel things that are not straightforward to process. You could just leave them to it, or you could go over and introduce yourself in a heavy-handed way that comes across as a warning both to him, and to her.

After you are spotted trying to take a picture of them on your phone, you're only left with the latter option really.

You're not totally blind.
You do pick up on things. You notice she does a little flinch when you raise your voice, for instance. She never initiates sex any more.

Come to think of it, she never initiates anything any more. It's like she's just waiting for you to tell her what should happen next all the time. This infuriates you, and leads inevitably to you raising your voice again.

She's changed, so you change.
Somehow, over time, you have managed to turn charm into sarcasm, admiration into envy, protectiveness into paranoia.

You have to win every conversation, you have to have the last word, you have to *know*. It's an old friend from her old work, she says. She must have mentioned him before, you know, *Pete*. Don't be silly, she says when she sees your expression, he's not even straight.

But she hasn't mentioned him. And besides, she could turn anyone straight. Just look at her.

You make a choice.
You confront her. She cries and says, it's only ever been you. You like the tears, but wonder if they are enough. You find yourself with a choice: lovingly accept her reassurances, or throw an unopened can of chopped tomatoes at the double-glazed French windows.

It's toughened glass, and you only break one pane. This, you say, shows how silly a little thing it all is. But already she is on the phone, sob-dialling. Better not to talk to anyone till we've all calmed down, you say, with a restraining hand.

You love someone, you set them free.
You can see she's not 100% happy. You're not either, come to that. So it makes sense for you to move out for a while – better that way, so others don't misinterpret things. You didn't want to cause a scene, after all, what with her crying and her dad and brother getting all worked up, trying to knock the door down for no good reason.

But you're always with her, she knows that. It's what she wants.

You like to sit outside her house in a car.
Just sit there and smoke, maybe have a beer and listen to some choons. You see her peer out from behind a curtain every so often. Though she needs space, you know she's reassured by your quiet background presence.

When she's ready to come and talk, you'll be there. Just need to get things back to where they were, back to where they should be.

The neighbours are a different matter, though. And it's not so easy when one of those cunts calls the police. 'How can I "harass someone in their own home" when I'm not even in their home?' you keep asking. 'And anyway, it's my home too.'

Well, it was.

You learn how to let yourself in and out of a car boot.
That way, you can be with her on her dates with this new Dave bloke. They never know you're there, of course, until the muscles cramps have you crying out in agony. It's what you do for love though, isn't it? That and six months, plus a Level 5 fine.

You reflect, you grow, you wait.
There's a lot of time in here to think about things. You know now there were moments when you tried too hard. When you didn't see her point of view. When you rushed to judgement or jealousy. There are things you'll do differently next time, ways you'll love her better.

There's a woman in here who's helping you to talk about your feelings. Get perspective on your pain, she calls it. It helps. You can see how things must have come across now. And you'll be a better person for her when you're done.

Because what can never change is what you and she mean to each other. You know there have been issues, you know you did wrong. But you're dying in here, and it wouldn't kill her to remind you just once that she needs you as much as you need her.

Otherwise, what's the point of you?

MINDFULNESS

The scene: a lunch party, somewhere in south-west London. The meal over, most of the guests have spilled out into the host's capacious back garden, leaving Rog and his sister Annabelle to catch up in the kitchen. Sounds of adult laughter and performative chat intermittently filter back to them from outside. Rog has come alone, while Annabelle is with her two children – Harry, 6, and Polly, 4. Music of a not quite placeable but achingly trendy sort plays in the background. Possibly lounge grime.

'So he was saying, right, we spend so much time directing our energy *outwards*. You know?'

'Right, right. Hold on, Rog, sorry. *Harry and Polly, go out and play in the garden for a bit, will you? They've put some toys out for you on the lawn there.*'

'. . . But how much of our intentionality ever gets pointed *inside?*'

'Right. *Harry, outside now! And leave the washing machine controls alone.* Sorry, Rog.'

'You know, sis, how much energy do we ever really put into understanding *ourselves*?'

'Absolutely. Tell me about it!'

'The inside of our skulls. Our *souls*.'

'Arseholes? Who? The other people on the retreat? *HARRY*!'

'Ha! No no. Our *souls*.'

'Sorry Rog, sorry – got a bit distracted there. Harry seems intent on sticking his Harry Potter wand in the cat's . . .'

'And when Master said that, it just suddenly hit me. That's *exactly* what I've been doing – you know, just pinballing through life, getting bounced from one thing to the next.'

'Oh yeah, totally. Like a, like a . . . pinball.'

'Exactly! Just being acted on by external forces. A bit like that cat.'

'Oh God! *Harry and Polly, will you please leave that cat alone! I really don't think it wants to wear my sunglasses right now.*'

'Just blowing about in the wind, drifting from one tempestuous love affair to the next, taking on whatever PAs and other gigs my agent comes up with, without ever really asking myself: how does this really, you know, *sit* . . . ?'

'*And no, I don't want to wear them now either Harry, thank you! Not now that you've buried them in the litter tray. Why can't you go outside?* Sorry, Rog, sorry. Not sure bringing the kids to this thing was such a great idea. I like your shades by the way.'

'Oh thanks, sis! They were a gift from Luciana, before we broke up? Some sort of off-label US-only limited edition, or something? You know, she's in couture so she gets access to all that stuff.'

'Very nice. *Polly, darling, do you want to come up on my lap? Then Harry won't be able to keep doing those annoying bunny-ears to you, will he?*'

'Hey Polly! Aw, sis. Just look at your little girl. She's so *here-and-now.*'

'You can say that again.'

'So, where was I?'

'Oh! You were suddenly thinking . . . You know . . . about, um . . . sitting?'

'Right. Exactly that. How often do I ever really ask myself: how does what I'm about to do, or *who* – because believe me, I've encountered some very beautiful people, models, actresses, whatever – how does this *sit* against the backdrop of eternity? You know? How does this . . . how will this . . . *sit?*'

'*How will* you *sit, Polly? Just choose one position and stick to it. My knees can't take all that jigging about.*'

'And that perspective, that insight of Master's . . . That was just one among so many! The whole time was just peppered

59

with these little explosions, these sort of spiritual lightbulbs that just kept flashing on in my mind, illuminating whole areas of consciousness I'd never really thought about before.'

'Wow. Rog. I mean, yes! *Well the cat's gone out into the garden now, Harry, and I really can't blame it.*'

'When you have to just sit and observe silence in stillness, sis, space itself just *ceases to be* somehow. And time too, in a very real sense, you know? Your mind, your spirit can fly free of the body. And suddenly you get to meet this extra-ordinary character called . . . *you*! You should try it some time!'

'*No. Harry, NO! Get your head out of the cat flap NOW! Play with something else. Please. There's a massive box of Lego they've got out for you there* . . . Sorry, Rog. So how long did you have to sit in one place?'

'Basically you meditate from dawn to dusk, with just a few breaks for food and stretching and stuff. It's agony on the back. But as Master says, "Embrace your sweet pain . . ."'

'Wow. So what did you find out about yourself? *Harry, just make do with the Lego that's there. I'm sorry if there aren't any more jumbo wheels, you'll just have to use your imagination and build what you can.*'

'See, that's it right there, isn't it? I realised that I'm just like Harry.'

'Not still shitting in swimming pools, I trust.'

'No no!'

'Or someone whose favourite joke is still that rhyme about how, *in nineteen seventy-four, the monkeys went to war . . .*'

'Eh?'

'*They had no guns so they used their bums, in nineteen seventy-four?* Repeated ad nauseam. From 5.15am.'

'Ha! Nice one, Harry! No, I'm like Harry because I've got a lovely big box of Lego in front of me, metaphorically speaking, full of all sorts of colourful, useful stuff. Yet all I can think is, "Why aren't there more jumbo wheels?" See? We always want . . . Correction, *I* – let me take responsibility for my thought, not try and wriggle out of it by putting it on everyone else (that's another thing I learned by the way) – *I* realised that *I* always want what *I* haven't got.'

'Oh right. Well, yes. Sleep in my case.'

'Whereas happiness or flourishment or whatever . . .'

'*Polly – please stop putting your Little Live Pet in my face! I know it wants to say hello, and I do too. But with all that chirping it's quite hard to hear uncle Rog's story.*'

'Happiness, sis . . . is just . . . *wanting what you've already got.*'

'*Polly, are you doing the poo dance? Shall we see if we can find the loo?* Sorry, Rog, I'm just not really used to these adult chats any more.'

'No worries, sis. You do your thing.'

'It sounds fascinating, anyway. How long were you actually there for?'

'Well the whole thing lasts fourteen days. It's known as the Fortnight of Gracious Silence. You're just stuck out in this massive old house with Master in the middle of the wilds of Dorset somewhere.'

'Is it a Buddhist thing? *Harry, pull your bottoms up! No one wants to see that.*'

'Somewhat. Master says it's a sort of blend of traditions. That's another thing I learned – how we all have this need to put labels on things.'

'Right, right.'

'You know. Am I Buddhist? Republican? Vegan? Are you a Remainer or a Neo-Nazi or a Suffragette, or whatever? These labels really just limit who we can be.'

'"Mummy that Drinks" is the one that seems to be following me around a lot at the mo.'

'Mmm.'

'Are you OK, Rog? You seemed miles away just then.'

'*Silence.* The sound of. Disconcerting isn't it? Just letting the emptiness flow into the space around us, without surrendering to our terrible urge to fill it with babble.'

'*Polly, are you sure you don't need a poo?*'

'That's it, yeah. Poo, basically. We fill our minds with banter and trivia to block out the things we really feel. You know, our innermost fears and desires.'

'I honestly don't think I've had the energy for an innermost fear or desire for some years. *Polly, if you really don't want the loo, then take your hands out of your pants darling, there's a good girl.*'

'Yeah, it's not always easy to hear what the self really has to say . . . *to the self*. And of course on retreat you've got no access to phones. No TV or music. No pubs or booze.'

'Wow. All alone for fourteen days! Sounds like bliss. *Harry, leave Polly alone! She's too small for you to ride around on her like that.*'

'Well, it was tough, actually, sis. It's supposed to be like, total silence, remember. You're not even supposed to speak to your co-meditators. And that was hard because, well, some of them obviously recognised me?'

'What, from that reality thing you did on Channel 5? Surely not. *Polly, stand up darling. Harry, enough now! Just look at her face – she's absolutely terrified!* Sorry, Rog . . . So you're supposed to unplug for the whole time? No Instagram, no Netflix, no internet?'

'Right. It's like a complete digital detox. You're like . . . completely off grid.'

'And you held out for fourteen days? Without your phone?'

'Well, give or take. I've got a few sponsorships in the pipe-line, so obviously I had to keep an open line to my agent . . . But basically, yeah. I "drank deep of the noble cup of serene solitude", as Master likes to say.'

'*Polly. Pick up those mango pieces! Oh God, you're a mess. Wipes! Where are my wipes?* So how long did *you* actually stay silent for, Rog?'

'Ah. Look at them.'

'*Oh God, what are they doing now?*'

'Nothing! Chill, sis! I mean *look at them*: Children.'

'Tell me about it.'

'So innocent. So pure. So . . . *of-the-moment.*'

'*Harry! Give Polly her Babybel back! Don't you dare scoff it. I mean it, Harry. Harry! Right. HARRY, YOU COME RIGHT HERE RIGHT NOW!*'

'Exactly! *Right here, right now.* Children are so mindful. They have no sense of the past or the future, they're just 100% focused on savouring the gift of the present moment.'

'*He'll be savouring the gift of no TV or iPad in a minute, if he doesn't get down off that window-ledge THIS VERY MOMENT.*'

'Exactly. *This* very moment. Not that moment, or any other moment. *This* one! Hey – I *love* talking to you, sis! You're so intuitive. So centred. So *grounded.*'

'Thanks! I mostly feel ground down, but thanks. And well done you! Fourteen days of silence, that's really something.'

'Well not quite the full fourteen. But then, I'm a quick learner. I mean, I got through *A Course in Miracles* in a week – some people spend decades on it! And as I say, I had some commitments.'

'*Put that down Polly! That's not a toy, that's a* . . . designer lemon squeezer. So . . . how much of the retreat did you actually do in the end, did you say, Rog. Rog?'

'Well it's more about quality than quantity, you know?'

'Right.'

'And I found you can really get a feel of the experience from a couple of afternoons.'

'Ah.'

'Plus the bedding was really scratchy? And you know, with my frantic schedule . . .'

'Yeah, I know. You've really got your hands full. *Harry and Polly – come on guys, we need to get our hats and coats on, and start heading back – it's school and pre-school tomorrow. And that means homework and packed lunches. And we still haven't done our costumes for World Book Day, have we?*'

'Yah. It's hard to be mindful when your head's full of stuff. You'll see what I mean once you're back at work, sis.'

'__'

NEAR MISS

The crazy golf was dinosaur-themed. It was right by a busy dual carriageway. They'd passed it often on the way home, and always said they'd go there one day.

The children were fighting in the back as Paula parked.

'*Stop looking at me*!' shouted the three-year-old boy. 'I *didn't*,' said the five-year-old girl. The three-year-old started crying.

Greg leaned round and snapped at his daughter. 'You always blame me! *It's not fair*!' she howled back, and burst into tears.

Paula manoeuvred the car to a halt, then turned to him, incredulous. 'Did you not just hear what I said?'

'What?'

'I said I don't feel I have anything to look forward to.'

'I'm sorry you feel like that.'

'I said that, and *you didn't even respond*.'

'—'

'*How do you think that makes me feel?*'

Another howl from the back seat.

'Let's get out,' he said suddenly.

They queued for their putters. The three-year-old would only use an adult-size club, which was almost taller than him.

A *T Rex* roared on cue. Everyone else was in a nuclear unit like theirs: two parents, two or three young children, sometimes with a grandparent or a comedy uncle or a cool aunt.

At each hole they waited in line, while the family in front refereed squabbles and retrieved orange balls from flower beds. Then they did the same.

Once more the five-year-old dropped her ball into the lurid-green moat surrounding the animated pterodactyl. Behind them in the queue, two boys fenced dangerously with their sticks. The roar of the traffic was deafening.

'Happy anniversary!' said Greg, to no one.

It was almost time to leave the playground. Neither had exchanged anything other than functional phrases since the row at the crazy golf. 'You got a quid for the meter?' 'Pass the wipes.' 'Watch his finger in the door!'

It occurred to Greg, as it often did in these situations, that he couldn't really remember what he was supposed to be angry with his wife *about*. He had adopted *an attitude* of anger, perhaps, as a pre-emptive defence against the obviously rather more substantial sense of grievance which she was currently nursing and which she would duly be able to articulate so effectively.

He nursed his own portfolio of grievances, of course he did, ready to be wheeled out when the occasion demanded. But there were tatty, half-forgotten things – like the patronising way she had told him not to bother doing the online grocery shop any more as she'd only have to go through it all afterwards and undo all his choices ('*seven kinds of crisp?!*'). Or the time she didn't even notice he'd tidied the kids' sock drawers. Or the time she didn't thank him for topping up the screenwash.

But he kept his powder dry because (a) he genuinely wanted to let go of all this crap and (b) he suspected she had stockpiled her own collection of far more pointed and deadly grievances about him, and the thought of this underground arsenal of righteous resentment scared the bejesus out of him.

So it would be he who would begin the process of truth and reconciliation, and she who would duly sign off on each of the necessary steps of confession and contrition. There were – admittedly rare – instances where he might have plausibly held out for the moral high ground, but in practice this almost never happened. Whatever the ins and outs of any specific wrangle, he believed secretly but utterly in his wife's essential moral and emotional superiority, and ultimately only one thing mattered: was she planning on leaving him? If still not, then ultimately any penance or apology was a small price to pay.

All in all, it was a familiar process, and he was suddenly anxious to start sooner rather than later. It was Sunday night after all, and pushing teatime without resolution did not bode well for any *détente conjugale* later on. Otherwise they might actually have to *watch Modus* or *Borgen* or *The Bridge* or whatever the latest lugubrious Nordic whydunnit was.

'I'm sorry.'

'What for?'

'I don't mean to ignore what you're saying. I'm just knackered.'

'You're always knackered. That's your excuse for everything.'

'Well I am.'

'What about—'

'I know. And you are too. I know. More than me no doubt. But I do care about what's happening to you, how your job's going and everything, you know I do.'

He felt his phone vibrate urgently. He wanted to tell her that he was purposely ignoring it, but was not sure she'd be impressed.

She said: 'I just feel that work takes all the best bits of you . . . and we're left with the dregs.'

'Come on, that's not fair.'

His phone vibrated again.

'Yesterday, when you went to call your mum, you dialled 9 for an outside line!'

'Well, that's just force of habit.'

'Exactly. And yet you can't even stand the place half the time, to hear you go on about it.'

'I just find the kids so difficult at the moment. You're much better at it than me.'

This line was a gambit, an attempt to assess the progress of *rapprochement*. In the event, his optimism proved premature. (He should have remembered his wife's pet hate of broad-sheet columns by middle-class dads going on about how hard it was to look after small children, while their wives silently got on with keeping the whole show on the road, just as they had always done.)

'You only see them when they're at their most fractious because you don't get home in time to actually *be* with them?' It sounded like a question, but he had no answer.

So the conversation proceeded, two steps forward and one step back, until she invited him to consider the fate of Mr Leslie at number 54, who in fact lived now *not* at number 54 but in the camper van parked *opposite* number 54 because his wife had got so sick of him letting her down all the time.

'But he's an alcoholic and a gambling addict!'

'I saw you give the kids scratchcards yesterday.'

It was the chink he had so desperately wished for, and great spiky shafts of winter sun began to blaze through it.

'I topped up the screenwash this morning. *And* I built that garden bench.'

'Only because the mice had started living in the pack-aging! That was a present for my fortieth – three years ago!'

'Don't tell me you're forty!' he essayed with cheeky chivalry. 'You don't look a day over fabulous!'

Thus they powered through the phases of their domestic peace process. Paula itemised the specifics of his crapness, and Greg both acknowledged these *and* asked for various additional offences to be taken into consideration. She smiled at last, and he in turn secured an assurance that the phrase 'I've got nothing to look forward to' had been less an existential statement of marital despair on her part, and more a catastrophising expression born of her deep frustration with his weekend shortcomings. Shortcomings which – as he had already stated and was happy to reiterate for the record – he fully acknowledged and gladly pledged to improve on in the coming days. But – in a rhetorical move he was trialling for the very first time – he asked not to be judged by his mere words in this matter, but by his future *actions.*

Somehow they had ended up with an arm around each other.

Millie, the five-year-old, now sidled over from the monkey bars. 'Look everyone!' she cried out to the playground at large. 'Take a picture of Mummy and Daddy cuddling!' Stan, the three-year-old, looked up from the roundabout he was pushing – why do they never actually want to *ride* on the thing? – and giggled. Other parents looked away.

'You being affectionate to me is so unusual Millie wants to capture the moment,' said Paula. 'And everyone else is thinking it must be a rare break from the violence.'

'*Mummy and Daddy sitting in a treeee!*' Millie taunted. 'K.I.S.S.I.N.G!'

'Look, we're the lucky ones,' she said. 'We've got the children. We've got each other. We've got our health. We've got a nice house. Decent jobs. We're rich in the ways that count.'

Over by the toddler swings, a woman in a wheelchair sat taut and silent as her little boy implored her to push him higher, faster.

'I know this. I do.'

'Well you've got a funny way of showing it.'

Over the road, on the other side of the busy junction, he made out an ominous scene. One car had stopped abruptly in front of another in the middle of the road, its hazard lights flashing savagely. The man in the first car was walking round the back of it and taking photos with his phone, shaking his head pointedly and muttering vengefully in the direction of the car behind him. In that car sat another, older man, inert and guilty-looking, arms locked on the steering wheel. The rest of the traffic threaded its respectful way around them.

Greg shivered with silent relief at his own near miss.

LISTING TO PORT

SATURDAY
Alka Seltzer
Vit B tabs (ones that fizz)
Coffee
Red Bull
Doritos
Eggs
Sausages (thick ones)
Mail/Mirror/FourFourTwo

TUESDAY
Smints
Mouthwash
Nice boxers
Bananas
Condoms
Guardian/Economist/Vanity Fair/TLS
Get cash out (loads)
Condoms

FRIDAY
Condoms
3 bottles red wine (min £12 each)

Big pack spaghetti
2 medium onions
Olive oil
3 garlic cloves (how many bulbs = 1 clove?)
500g lean minced beef
90g chestnut mushrooms
400g can chopped tomatoes
Hot beef stock (or cold and reheat?)
Worcestershire sauce
Ground black pepper
Sea salt
Tomato puree
Freshly grated parmesan (to serve)
1tsp oregano

Teaspoons!
Decent plates
Knives
Forks

Daffodils
Vase for flowers
Wine glasses

~~CDs? (timeless but not cheesy – Motown?)~~
~~CD player~~
~~Speakers~~

Subscribe to Spotify (no ads)
Get laptop fixed

1 kg potty puree (dried herbal incense thing)
Bin bags
Dishcloths, wipes, tissues

Shake n vac stuff
Kitchen roll
Nice duvet cover/Pillow cases/Sheets
Toilet bleach x 4
Handgel
Antibacterial cleaners, all kinds
Dry-clean rugs? Curtains?

Gin (NOT Tescos own)
Fever Tree
Posh ice cream
Baileys
Croissants
Coffee
Strawberry jam
Blueberries, raspberries etc
Milk

Condoms
Furry handcuffs??

Polyfilla

WEDNESDAY
Nice card or nice writing paper
Perfume (expensive)
Fancy hand conditioner stuff? (posh)
Earrings or nice bracelet? (both?)
Box and bubble-wrap
Post Office – send Express? Get her to sign?

Send flowers

THURSDAY
Call EE – check phone working

FRIDAY
Call EE
Get Cosmopolitan/Marie Claire etc
Library – get that *Mars & Venus* book

SATURDAY
Call EE
Call mum

SUNDAY
Lager x 12
Wine box (red) (or white)
Tissues
Wotsits (big pack)
Chocolate milk
Large bar Dairy Milk
Pepperami
Potato waffles
Chocolate milk stuff
Pot noodles
Coffee!!
Band-Aids
Savlon
Doughnuts
Bottle of port (Tesco's own)

MINUTES OF DIVISIONAL BOARD MEETING Q4/18

Date: 11 November 2018
Venue: Commerce House
Time of meeting: 14.00 – 15.05

Board members present:
Kieran Detton (KD), Group MD, EMEA
Rob Starky (RS), Divisional CFO
Morwenna Orson (MO), acting Divisional MD
Jon Whitehouse (JW), Group Sales Director
Toby Ushant (TU), Head of IT and Data
Gabby Hinsen (GH), Chief HR Officer
Corinne Rudd (CR), minute-taker and Deputy House Counsel.

Apologies: Tom Wiseman (TW), Global CEO

1. Approval of the minutes of the previous Divisional Board meeting, Q3/18

Chairing the meeting in her capacity as acting Divisional MD, MO referred the board to the minutes of the meeting held on 15

September 2018. Said minutes were approved and seconded. KD asked that board papers and minutes be circulated further in advance in future. MO apologised for the delay, which she said had been due to illness.

Actions from the last meeting were discussed: all had been satisfactorily completed, with the exception of the presentation of the new divisional business development strategy. JW asked that this action be held over till the following quarter, by which point he would have finalised the new budgeting structure for EMEA, and a more realistic projection of goals against costs could be formulated. KD commented that this sounded like a far more credible excuse than 'ladies' troubles' or whatever MO's issue had been, and the board approved JW's request.

2. Words of welcome

KD noted that TU and MO had hugged each other warmly at the start of the meeting, and he wanted to know why he didn't get a hug from MO too. TU replied that he and MO were old friends. KD responded that he was still concerned whether this was an appropriate style of greeting in today's post-Weinsteinian workplace, especially if he couldn't get in on the action. Winking in GH and CR's general direction, he added that he knew he would never get a hug off either of them, so he hadn't bothered asking.

JW said that he'd like to take the opportunity at this point to thank KD for his brave words. With all the talk of #metoo and accusations of harassment flying around and poor Cliff Richard, it was hard for men to know where they stood these days, he said. RS agreed. Men simply didn't know what they could get away with any more, he added. GH reminded RS that he had recently married; RS replied that he was of course speaking hypocritically [sic].

MO suggested, with GH's agreement, that a good rule of thumb was to consider whether an action was an abuse of your position, and/or likely to leave the other person feeling embarrassed, humiliated or used. JW asked her if she'd ever attended the Annual Divisional Sales Awards. GH said that she had attended once, and the evening would be seared in her memory for ever after.

KD said that women had a right to be treated respectfully, even the ugly ones. He added that this was a joke, and should not be minuted. GH said this sort of remark was precisely the problem; men made fine speeches on the topic but their underlying attitudes remained unchanged. RS said that, *au contraire*, GH's words were precisely the problem. GH asked him to elaborate. RS said it was clear that if women had a sense of humour we wouldn't all be in such a mess. At this point the meeting briefly paused so that RS, KD and JW could chortle among themselves.

KD now commented that, in all seriousness, and setting jokes aside, it was important to note that most men were keen to do the right thing, but many were confused about whether they could still have a go if one looked like she was gagging for it. But MO observed that it was extraordinary how, even now, after everything that had been revealed, men were still finding a way to make the #metoo narrative about them.

Appearing to ignore this (and staring at MO's breasts all the while), KD next said that he was sure that all present would agree with him that things had moved on significantly. There had been no accusations of men disrespecting women on his watch, after all, and he was proud to preside over a harassment-free workplace. At this point the meeting paused once more, so that MO, CR and GH could briefly snort with scorn among themselves.

RS asked for the meaning of this unfeminine braying, and MO and GH asked if any of the men present were familiar with [name redacted] on the third floor. KD pronounced him a top bloke, while JW said 'Fat Bob' had never knowingly been out-drunk by anyone. GH asked if the board were familiar with any of his other nicknames. When the male directors shook their heads, GH said they included 'Touchy-Feely', 'Spider Man' and 'Sex Pest'.

KD noted that, isolated incidents aside, things really had moved on in the industry very significantly. He said that when he had started out, hateful phrases like 'menstrual mafia' and 'asking for it' and 'feminist' were thrown around casually; today you really had to go out of your way to hear such talk, even at the golf club. GH replied that 'feminist' wasn't a hate-word. KD replied that he knew where she was coming from, but it was probably best not to minute that. He then asked if he was going to have to hold up a sign which said 'only joking' at the end of every sentence.

MO said that, while it was wonderful to hear the company was making great strides on this issue, there was still some way to go. GH said she had to agree, adding that Fat Bob was hardly an isolated case and there remained several male staff members who had not altered their sexist or demeaning behaviour to women in years. When RS asked why, if so, the women in question had never complained, MO answered that there had indeed been several complaints made by women to their line managers, who all happened to be male, and no further action had been taken.

KD asked MO to expand on the implication of her last remark. MO said it was surely obvious. KD said it was not obvious; furthermore, he reiterated the board's recently agreed consensus that great strides had already been made on the issue. It was worth noting, he added, that as a society we are very much where we are; in addition, the situation was one which was, he noted, very much what it was. KD also reminded MO that she was currently only acting up to her new role, and wondered if she really had the right mindset to step up on a permanent basis.

3. Acting MD's report

MO now presented the acting MD's report to the Board. She talked about her successful migration of the Division's entire back-end e-commerce functionality to the Cloud, and updated the Board on the progress of her three-year strategic plan to pivot the Division's commercial activities to a subscription-based payment model, a bold and innovative approach which had already resulted in an 11% increase over forecast revenue year-on-year. At this point, MO asked KD why he was looking at her strangely. KD replied that when MO presented, he noticed that her chin had a way of trembling ever so slightly, and it was really pretty. RS and JW added that they had both noticed this, and both also found it attractive.

4. Adjournment

At this point MO asked for an extraordinary adjournment of the board meeting on the grounds of sudden illness. KD asked what the problem was. MO said that she was experiencing menstrual cramps. KD winced expressively, and said there was no need to enter into the gruesome details. He added that he did wonder if the whole equal pay hadn't gone a bit too far, especially when one gender was always taking time out for, you know. MO said that actually she was fine, although KD's reaction was instructive. KD asked what she meant. MO replied that she had arranged for the current meeting to be live-streamed to the Division's 373 employees, 67.3% of whom were women, and she would leave it to others to explain.

The agenda was suspended at this point, and the meeting adjourned.

EMBARRASSMENT OF RICHES

On Happy FM they'd announced a prize of £30,000 for the first person in the city to locate a tiny golden Happy FM Bear. A new clue to its whereabouts was broadcast every hour, just after the news and travel. But the children went off the idea of bear-searching within a few minutes of realising that the prize wouldn't be instantly forthcoming, unlike all the Easter egg hunts and treasure trails they'd ever taken part in. And besides, Matt had promised them a morning of soft play.

The heavy rains of May had given way to the heavy heat of June; it was a day for being outside. KidZone was dark and cool inside, and completely empty. There was just Shenika, whom they found mopping the cafeteria floor. She looked up with a start when she heard Matt, Jon and Milly wade in.

'So . . . no one comes to a soft-play when the weather's this nice?' he attempted. He and Shenika were vaguely familiar with each other from his many visits with the children to this low-lit barn of curvy slides and ball pits and cushioned ramps.

She nodded to the floor. 'Thought I'd get on with this now,' she said, flicking the mop handle at the lino with weary ease.

Matt liked Shenika. Her facial expression tried always for the armoured officiousness you'd doubtless need to survive in a world of screaming kids and fed-up parents, but a pinkly vulnerable warmth was always peeping through. She was likeable, despite her best efforts.

Matt paid – £2 for two-year-old Jon, £4 for four-year-old Milly, £4 for himself – and signed the clipboard. They were Shenika's first, perhaps only, customers of the day.

'That'd do nicely,' said Shenika, nodding at the latest bulletin about the Happy FM Bear and the £30k. 'Thirty grand.' She had turned back to the yellow bucket on wheels and the smell of disinfectant. 'Wouldn't have to do this any more.'

'What would you do with thirty grand, though?'

She looked up. In this hot empty space, without the usual screaming crowd and against the overpowering hygiene smell, the question seemed oddly intimate, even impertinent.

She looked back down to her mopping. 'Stick some away. Get all that interest.'

'You'd still have to work though, that's the thing,' he said. 'And rates are poor right now. You'd really need a million to give up everything for good.' She gave him an odd look.

Matt winced to himself. He knew suddenly quite a bit about investment strategies and interest rates and early retirement plans himself, because about three weeks ago he had anonymously won £973,578.81 on the lottery.

Jon was running round KidZone, heading for the Bob the Builder machine he loved. He heaved himself up next to Bob and sat triumphant in the cab of Scoop (or was it Muck? Or Dig?). Meanwhile Milly, a soft play veteran, had already thrown off her socks and sandals and was scaling the big cushioned zig-zag steps in the direction of the ballpit.

By the time Matt reached her, Milly had set up a production line and was making party food on an industrial scale. Yellow balls went into the pit for ice cream, red she kept on one side for jelly, the rest were rejected. Daddy's job was to fetch the many balls that had spilled out of the main pit into the mesh-lined alcoves round the side or rolled down the soft steps into the toddler area where the big plastic bricks were.

The knowledge of the money ate away at him. It wouldn't digest. Only his wife Sally knew the details. He could never have realised that wanting a lot of money could feel so different from having a lot.

But this was fun, no? Milly sat on the top step and giggled as Matt whizzed the rogue balls up to her. He was here right now, in the moment. *If only we have each other, then are we not rich indeed?*

Jon. Matt looked around. *Fuck.* Where's Jon? *Fuck. Joooooooon!!*

Matt staggered out of the soft play, ducking clumsily through the child-size mesh opening and back out into the cafeteria area, its floor still shiny-wet in patches from the mopping. The fire escape doors were wide open to the blaring sun to help the floor dry. Outside he scanned the bins, the loading bay, the alleyway leading so quickly to the busy main street. *Nothing no one nowhere.*

Matt had been to this brink many times before. He thought he'd lost Jon out in the road only that morning, when the plumber came and the front door got left ajar. But he would not feel sick, he would not believe, unless or until he had to. He could not even watch films about this sort of thing.

Ducking back inside, he saw that Shenika had heard his shouts and was jerking her head around with the look of one not used to sudden movements.

Just then, Jon padded out from behind the Bob the Builder machine with the insouciance of the child in the Temple. (*'Did you not know I would be about Mr Bernard Bentley's business?'*) Jon, with his muppet gait and blond Boris mop-top and mock-baleful expression. Jon with his precocious scootering skills and liberal sloppy kisses and his insistence that seals were a kind of bird.

Jon, with his untroubled pulse and heartbeat.

'Oh God. You gave me heart pains then.' Shenika shot Matt a look that was part relief, part accusation. And Matt thought: *What profiteth a man, if he gain the whole world but lose his two-year-old son under a bus?*

'Morrisons!' he said.

The money had not brought instant happiness. When Matt and his wife had first found out, they had sat down for a celebratory meal and ended up solemn and anxious.

Sally had cried at the thought of people she loved who had died too soon and never known such good fortune. People they could have helped, people with hard lives that could have been so different with a bit more cash. And Matt had realised that money can only make you happy if you have some idea of who you are or where your life is heading.

He had dreamed of money as ease; you had to have it to know it only made things more complex. A million was an abstract thing that was easily mistaken for a concrete thing.

There was the bewildering array of options that suddenly opened up, that did not so much liberate or exhilarate as dazzle and confuse. There was the fear of being the one who'd had it all but threw it away, like waking up after a piss-up to discover that you'd spunked it all on some dodgy pub deal involving timeshares and a racehorse.

And then of course there was the guilt that all of the above were absurd first-world, one-per-center anxieties that anyone in their right mind would kill to be wracked by.

The cafeteria in Morrisons had much to recommend it. The coffee was pretty good. It was all very cheap. The fish and chips were award-winning, apparently. And the place was a sort of unofficial drop-in centre for the local community.

Matt didn't work Thursdays now, so after a morning's soft play or playground supervision or swimming, he liked to come here with Milly and Jon for lunch. The kids knew the place, understood the protocols, liked the food, and would sit still-ish for twenty-five minutes making a mess for someone else to clear up. What was not to like?

Sally pointed out that there was plenty of food at home, that it was wasteful to eat out every single Thursday. In addition, he was giving the kids the unfair impression that she was austere, penny-pinching mum while he was expansive, fun-times dad.

Matt protested that Morrisons was cheap, and it wouldn't be that long before the children were both at school and these treats would no longer be possible. But the truth was that, with all that cash sitting ill-digested in the bank (several banks, actually), he struggled to see the point of saving money any more, or of chasing after discounts and money-off deals, or any of that reusing, reducing and recycling stuff they used to go in for.

He struggled to remember the point of the whole proud scrimping philosophy that had always underpinned their marriage. Scrimping was fun and righteous; it meant the allotment they'd put so much into and presents wrapped in newspaper and refusing to play the brand game. It meant making sandwiches for lunch and getting the bus to school instead of driving and saving up Clubcard points to pay for a treat trip to Legoland. It was anchored to an idea of sustainable family happiness.

But now that they could afford everything, what was the point of skimping on anything? Why not eat out every day? Why not get a cab instead of the bus? Why not hire a cleaner and a nanny and a gardener?

Why go to work at all, come to that? What price value now?

At the next table, a youngish man in a mobility buggy was telling his story to a man in his late seventies or early eighties who brought his wife in for lunch every day and always talked to everyone. Matt heard the younger man say, 'I've been in this for seventeen years. Bike accident' and 'Hospitals in Cyprus are no better' and 'I believe in fate'.

The older man's wife was in a wheelchair. She used to join in such chats but now her expression was fixed and her head lolled heavily to one side. Did the man look after her single-handed, Matt wondered? Did they have children? Matt always thought it the height of injustice that at the end of a long marriage and decades of parenting, one of you ended up having to spend your final years as carer for the other. Back to all that spoon-feeding and arse-wiping when probably all you wanted to do was sit down and watch some telly.

Just then a woman sat down at the next table. Listlessly, she held her plastic order number in her hand and stared blankly ahead. She wore a T-shirt that said 'YOLO'. From the branding on her top YOLO seemed to Matt to be a *thing*, some sort of meme or catchphrase he had never quite understood, like when young people say 'for the win' or all those 'one does not simply . . .' gifs with Sean Bean in.

So began the long trek homewards in the heavy heat. Matt was pushing Jon in the buggy, the boy's scooter balanced awkwardly on the buggy's handles. Milly had her scooter too, but she had gone all floppy and impossible, and their progress was halted every three or four paces when she discovered another 'ant-house' in the pavement. 'I am interesting in these!' she declared. 'Take a picture, Daddy! Take a picture!'

Around each crack in the pavement, ants had piled up earth to make nests. For Milly, discarding her scooter and pressing her cheek to the pavement, each nest up close – and there were many, many of them to come along the route home – offered a fascinating vista of microcosmic energy and bustling purpose.

Matt stepped wearily over his daughter, hooked her scooter to the buggy's handle bars alongside Jon's, and leant in to start pushing the heavy Phil and Ted two-seater up the long, steep street that led to their own road. Progress was slow. The buggy was heavy and cumbersome with the two scooters, and Milly's endless ant stops were infuriating.

Thursdays with the children. Dads didn't use to do this, did they? Certainly his own dad hadn't been expected to, and probably wouldn't have thought it his department anyway. But this was the real wealth, wasn't it? Time spent together. Only no one told you that childcare was much harder than grown-up work, or that it required reserves of selflessness and energy and initiative that were beyond Matt, leading to recurrent guilt, anxiety and resentment, and a desperate resolve to just *survive the day*.

Sally gave him pieces of advice that sounded so obvious and calm and sensible that Matt assumed they could be safely ignored – things like 'don't try and do too much', 'have a plan for the day and stick to it' and 'don't expect too much of them'.

It was only after a few Thursdays that Matt realised that Sally's words weren't idle truisms but vital survival lessons to be adhered to with extreme prejudice.

Matt saw each Thursday as a blank diary page that he filled with strips of colour ranging from white through to darkest black. The white bits represented the moments where he could be satisfied with his performance as a dad – efficient, well-organised, in the moment, selflessly in control; the darker strips were where he had ignored their needs, spent time checking his emails or reading football reports online, lost his temper, or failed to remember they were only two and four. Lots of things really.

Usually the day started off bright white with the can-do optimism and good intentions of morning, but as it wore on the strips turned to grey or darker, especially after lunch, when he was tired and Jon wouldn't sleep, and again before dinner, when they were hungry and ratty and so, frankly, was he. Some nights Sally worked late so Matt put them to bed on his own too, and these moments were often the darkest strips of all.

Today had not been too bad so far. Obviously there would be a blot in the copybook around the time he had lost Jon, OK both times, and there had been moments of irritability and impatience throughout the morning. But now Milly had halted again.

Milly, with her am-dram renditions of the songs from *The Greatest Showman* and her ridiculously expressive nostrils and her obsession with the Great Fire of London (which she said should have been called 'The Bad Fire of London' as there wasn't anything *great* about it). Milly, with her nightmares about grasshoppers and her goggles improvised from salami slices with eyeholes in and her tiny eczema-scarred arms. Milly, who had ignored his dozen shouted requests to find her shoes that morning on the grounds that *I have to build an igloo for my dolphin.*

Not for the first time as a parent, Matt meditated furiously on the word *tether*.

He recalled now the woman at the next table, slouching over her poached egg on toast. As Millie dawdled and dithered, Matt googled YOLO. Then, stiff and self-conscious, he lay full out on the pavement and angled his phone for a better ant-house shot.

LORD, IN YOUR MERCY

Lord,
We pray for the sick and infirm of our parish, and all who
are distressed in mind or body. Console those in pain or
discomfort, Father, and give strength and patience to those
who look after them.
    Lord, in your mercy . . .
    Hear our prayer.

As Betty sat writing the week's bidding prayers, she found
herself thinking about Father David, and wondering again if
she could really go through with this.

She and Father David had worked together on many
Parish Council events over the years, but they first became
really close on the way back from a visit to the shrine at
Walsingham the previous April.

Betty was very moved by the visit, and on the return journey she had sat alone at the back of the coach, quietly
tearful. Father David hauled himself along the swaying aisle
and sat down next to her, and soon she was crying with him
about her late husband, Pat. Father David soothed and
sympathised, and by the time the coach pulled into the car
park opposite the church, Betty was asleep on his shoulder.

Lord,
We pray for our priests and bishops, and for all those who
have made the courageous decisions to devote their lives to
You. Grant them the faith and strength to continue on
their path, and may they find support and encouragement
among those they serve.
Lord, in your mercy . . .
Hear our prayer.

Betty began to help Father David out in small ways – defrost-
ing his freezer, ironing his shirts, sewing on the occasional
button. Theirs was a chaste relationship, at least to start with,
in which the odd weekly meeting for coffee and a chat in
Sainsbury's – just to see how Betty was holding up – slowly
turned into a near-daily ritual. Topics ranged from Betty's
grief to thorny scriptural puzzles to a shared love of *Strictly*.

Soon they were meeting at the Presbytery, where Betty
took to bringing in food so she could cook Father David the
proper nourishing lunches he craved. A typical beans-on-
toast bachelor, he devoured her shepherd's pies, her
homemade chicken kiev, and her trademark salmon en
croûte, centrepiece of so many Catholic Ladies' Association
dos.

They say the way to a man's heart is through his stomach,
but Betty was just pleased to serve this man who did so much
for others. She loved to cook, and it took her mind off her
own troubles. Soon she had her own key.

Lord,
At this time of great division in the world, we ask you to
support the work of our political leaders, here and overseas.
Grant them the wisdom to make decisions that will lead to a
fairer society, and the courage to stand up against injustice
in all its forms.

Lord, in your mercy . . .
Hear our prayer.

While watching the news one evening – somehow they had graduated from lunch – Betty emerged from the kitchen to see Father David dressed not in his habitual cassock or his modest black jumper and grey trousers, but in rather trendy running gear.

Stripped of his usual formless garb, Father David turned out to have a surprisingly powerful-looking physique. (Betty couldn't help noticing). Big veins stood out on his arms, and his legs had an agreeable chunkiness to them.

Betty had not even looked at a man since Pat's untimely heart attack three years ago. But now here was this great gentle holy bear – with his gracious demeanour, his spiritual insights and those bottomless kind brown eyes. A man who was always ready to listen to her troubles or hear her confessions – mostly quite unnecessary, as he always told her.

Father David didn't look a bit like Pat, she couldn't help thinking. Pat who – though he had the kindest, loveliest eyes in the world – would have been the first to admit he was a touch on the scrawny side. But why even consider such things? And why now? And why had it felt so funny to think that Father David was just a few yards away, naked and steaming wet in his hot shower, while she fussed about with the cutlery and the tray for their TV dinner?

When he came back into the room, Father David wore a loose-fitting tracksuit with a towel around his neck, and a subtle musk infused the room from his still-damp skin. That night, she stayed to watch *The One Show*.

Lord,
We pray for all the holy souls who have died in the peace and love of the risen Lord. We think especially of all the

departed family and friends of the people of this parish, as
we take a moment to remember our own loved ones.

Lord, in your mercy . . .

Hear our prayer.

Late one morning in January, Betty let herself in to the
Presbytery with a big bag of groceries. It was Father David's
birthday, and she wanted to surprise him with his favourite
meal of toad-in-the-hole followed by lemon meringue pie.

Father David was nowhere to be found, and this was just
as she'd hoped – he was probably still finishing up a visit to
the hospital, where he was often called to administer the
Sacrament of the Sick. But Betty had barely begun chopping
the mushrooms when she heard a strange basso heaving
sound, repeated over and over, coming from, was it upstairs?

Betty had never left the ground floor of the Presbytery
before. She had done her best to prettify its stark masculine
decor with house plants and throws and a few prints of old
masters – nothing too extravagant and nothing inappro-
priate, of course, but it all helped to brighten up the place.

As she crept up the stairs, she saw that the first floor was
even more sparse and unloved than the ground floor had
once been. Bare wooden floors and stale magnolia walls
framed a corridor of many doorways. (Father David had told
her the house had six bedrooms in all, on its three floors. He
said he always felt guilty about all this being available for just
one single man. He often wished that he could have some
refugees come and live with him, he said, but the diocese
wouldn't allow it.)

She was still clutching her short, sharp vegetable knife as
she creaked up the stairs and tiptoed breathlessly towards the
source of the noise, which seemed to be the second doorway
on the left. A low animal noise, it sounded like now, and
slowly she relaxed her grip on the knife.

Father David lay on his bed. He wore a towelling dressing gown of an odd mustard shade. Betty in the doorway couldn't help smiling to herself, despite the situation, for this was a choice of clothing that only a relentlessly single and deeply unworldly man could think tasteful in any way. Her heart went into the room ahead of her.

Father David was wrapped in a loose ball, quietly howling to himself. She knew already, without him saying, that his mother – who had been seriously ill for several months – had just died. Betty went to him and asked if he was all right. He said he had a pain. But Betty wasn't stupid and she gave herself to him then and there because she had known that this this day was coming, and she had no more resistance left.

And so a bomb of intimacy exploded in her life, and this new proximity was so thrilling that neither could apparently find a good reason not to make love a second time, or a third, and very soon. And in this way, those tricky moments of guilty doubt that can prevent a shared impulse from turning into a clandestine habit were easily overcome.

Father David was ardent and grateful; Betty felt things she dared not express. She was patient and loving, and she was glad that this all helped to console him. But of course her conscience began roasting on its own tormented spit even before they had finished the first time, which moment was, like Father David, not long in coming.

Lord,
We pray for our teachers, and all who work selflessly to equip our children with the qualities and skills they will need to face the future. May they be inspired by the loving patience of the greatest teacher of all, Your Son, as they work to help others become their best selves.

Lord, in your mercy . . .
Hear our prayer.

Father David knew nothing about sex really, and almost as little about women. So, although not especially experienced in the ways of love herself, Betty was able to show him a few things. And he could not have been a more enthusiastic and responsive student, always ready to revise a tricky learning point or to put a new skill to the test.

There was a tenderness here, and a happiness of sorts, tucked away in this nest they made for themselves up in the smallest of the guest bedrooms on the second floor, where no one could ever reach them, not even themselves perhaps.

But it would never be straightforward for a woman like Betty to be with a man like Father David, and indeed the only way she could make things work was to divide herself into two, and to forbid each part to have knowledge of the other. Betty sometimes had to switch between selves more than once in the course of an afternoon, especially if Father David's pain came hard upon him.

And Betty knew that he must have wrestled with all this too, as priests no doubt have to struggle with all sorts of weighty things that ordinary parishioners can't begin to fathom. But they never really discussed it, and Father David had a funny way of never showing any signs of struggle, except perhaps that he whistled and sang around the house a lot more.

But out in the church, the other women knew. Betty could tell. She knew from the small catch in the voice of old Miss DeCarlo as they arranged the flowers together, from a pointed glance the Bellingham sisters shot each other one coffee morning, from Sally Duggan's subtly pointed references to 'poor Father David's time of need'.

And now Betty's soul began to twist a little more in the wind, because she both loved Father David and knew that loving him this way was wrong, and she didn't know how she was supposed to feel both these things at once. Certainly not in front of old Miss DeCarlo, with whom she'd been arranging flowers for twenty years and who had a way of looking at you that cut right to the heart of things.

Ironically, the one person to whom Betty might have turned to to help work this all out was the man who now loved to pull her close so he could kiss her eyebrows, and tickle her neck with a whisper of hot breath, and lick the heady metallic aroma of her coarsely shaven armpits, and gently stroke the back of her knees with his thumbs. And the worst of it was that if he did these things so well now, it was all just as she had shown him. (Not the armpits, that was his idea, and she didn't really like it.)

Sensing her trouble, Father David offered to hear her confession, but they were in bed in the afternoon at the time, and the ironies of the situation quickly defeated her.

Lord,
We pray for all those who suffer from a sense of isolation, whether through illness, bereavement, discrimination or imprisonment. May they find consolation in your loving presence, and in the companionship of friends, relatives and neighbours.
    Lord, in your mercy . . .
    Hear our prayer.

As time went on, Betty began to feel less and less herself. There seemed to be no time any more for the things she'd loved most about being with Father David – doing the crossword, discussing the meaning of parables, working through their respective sadnesses, watching Wimbledon, debating the pros and cons of women priests(!), all the give-and-take of a happy, stimulating companionship.

In giving herself to him, she had thought that they were setting a seal on their love. She knew it was technically wrong, but she had also dared to wonder if it wasn't profoundly *right* on some deeper level that would one day be recognised and justified. Priests could marry in other churches, after all, and they were allowed to stay married if they converted to Catholicism. Betty had even allowed herself to imagine that she and Father David were like a pair of early apostles, professing in secret – for fear of persecution – a love that would one day be revealed as the triumphant truth.

Father David, meanwhile, wanted Betty whenever he saw her. He would make up errands and messages to get her round to the Presbytery and up to the guest bedroom again. It was uncanny, how quickly he could turn from one role to another. She saw how he switched effortlessly from pious, eyes-closed sermoniser to panting, eyes-closed lover. He could be off the altar and off with his trousers in minutes.

They alarmed her, these rapid transitions. They made her wonder sometimes if Father David's prayerful way wasn't so much him as a costume he wore, something he could slip off as easily as the cassock that he would throw in haste to the bedroom floor (a thing she hated to see; she would always get up and hang it in another room).

Betty would have liked to discuss these things with Father David. But the more they slept together, she noticed, the less he wanted to talk to her. She thought about praying too. But she felt that she had disqualified herself from the consolations of prayer through her actions, especially as those actions showed no sign of ceasing. Her sense of sin was compounded both by its knowing repetition and because of who it involved: to her devout mind, sleeping with a priest was doubly wrong, like shooting a police officer.

She thought of going to see another priest, or a counsellor, someone in a different parish. But she knew from Father David that the world of priests was a small one, and she couldn't bear the thought of betraying him, even accidentally.

And so she said nothing, while Father David went on with his demands and never seemed to notice that she seemed sadder and quieter than before. Or perhaps he did, but priests have a way of putting a brave face on things, as no doubt they have to, and Father David was still able to sleep soundly at night. Betty knew this, because sometimes she lay there staring at his sated snoring form till dawn, when she would silently get up and sneak back to her own forgotten life.

> Lord,
> We offer our prayers in support of the private intentions of all here today. We ask you to hold our prayers in your heart, O Lord, and to guide us safely through life's challenges.
> Lord, in your mercy . . .
> Hear our prayer.

The situation might have continued indefinitely, except that Father David started to seem irritated by Betty's attentiveness, and to adopt a much colder, more distant way with her. He was worried whether a man in his position should be seen to be devoting so much pastoral care in one direction, he said. Apparently there had been mutterings of concern from the diocese that he was indulging in 'a particular friendship', he said.

Father David began to reduce Betty's visits. He didn't always return her calls now, or he fobbed her off with last-minute appointments that they both knew he'd just invented. When pressed, he told her that it would be best for both of them if they could get back to their former, more conventional friendship, one which befitted their respective positions in the parish.

Betty agreed with this in principle, it was actually what she wanted. But it was confusing too, because in their previous friendship she didn't remember him phoning her very late at night, tearful and a bit drunk, to say that the pain was too much and he needed her right now, please, just to talk. And her heart would melt and she would go to him, and of course it would happen again. Then he'd avoid her for days afterwards again.

Betty decided that she had to do something proactive about the situation. She knew he'd ignore her if she called or texted, so she decided to let herself in with the key she still had, the one he'd never asked to have back. She thought she'd cook him a nice steak and ale pie, and they could just sit and talk things through, put it all behind them, get back to being friends.

So late one Thursday morning, she slipped into the Presbytery with a bag of groceries. She had just got the meat on a slow simmer and was rolling out the pastry when she heard anguished noises coming from above her. Betty forgot all her resolutions and rushed up to his room on the first floor, where she found him lying back on his bed, eyes closed, moaning loudly. She also found a half-naked Bellingham sister (the one that never married) sitting astride him, her face a picture of ecstatic shock.

Lord,
We pray for those who live in the shadows beyond the light cast by Your saving grace. Help us to remember that those who have lost the faith are Your creatures too, O Lord, and grant that they may one day know again the joy of the risen Jesus, who is our Salvation.
 Lord, in your mercy . . .
 Hear our prayer.

Betty slipped away from the scene, and from everyone. Finding Father David and the Bellingham sister together like that was like looking into a mirror that reflected her own sin back to her. She was more remorseful than ever, of course, but she was also very disappointed to discover how bitter and jealous she felt too. She had thought she and Father David had a special bond, but she could now see that he was just like a little boy with a clever new trick that he can't resist trying out on everyone.

She blamed herself. She imagined the expression of disapproval on her late parents' faces, and those sharp eyes of old Miss DeCarlo, and the little looks and mutterings of all the others, and she did not know how she could ever go back to church again. This was almost the most painful thing of all, because she loved church.

Betty thought of Pat, and how none of this would have happened if he'd still been around. Even if it had, she knew that he would have found a way to forgive her anyway, because that was just Pat.

Pat not being here just made her feel even worse, because there would never be anyone else in the world who could ever really see her *for her*, or who could ever really absolve her. Now it was as if she was grieving for Pat all over again from the start, only even more deeply and painfully. She lost days and weeks falling through the false floors of her pain, spending hours at his graveside, staring into space, mouthing silent words, weeding the already pristine grass.

The days and weeks blurred into a trance. Betty sleepwalked through work, ignored calls and messages from family and friends. But she held back from thoughts of suicide because she remembered a priest telling her at school that despair was the gravest sin of all. The sin of despair, the priest said solemnly, is the one sin that cannot be forgiven.

Betty smiled grimly at this memory, because the sins she'd committed with Father David, it seemed to her now, were all sins of despair.

Lord,
We pray for the work of the church around the world and
for Her missionaries, who bravely spread the word of God's
saving love. We pray especially for our own former parish
priest, Father David, in his new challenge as a missionary in
Guatemala.

Lord, in your mercy . . .
Hear our prayer.

Someone must have tipped the diocese off about Father
David, though you can be sure it wasn't Betty. Of course the
church did that church thing of moving the problem on
rather than actually dealing with it.

Betty inherited a little terrier from a housebound neighbour, and early every morning she walked it to the cemetery.
She took on extra shifts at the hospital whenever they were
going. Every night, she took scraps over to feed the foxes
behind the old tennis courts, walking her dog with an
exhausted stoop she'd never had before.

One day old Miss DeCarlo knocked on her door and said
she had a bone to pick with her. Betty looked panicked and
tearful. Miss DeCarlo said she was cross with Betty for being
such a bighead. A bighead? said Betty. Yes, said Mrs DeCarlo.
Very big-headed indeed. Because Betty must have done something really extraordinarily evil to think she was too grand or
special to deserve the forgiveness of the Lord. At this, Betty
smiled for the first time in a long time, because Miss DeCarlo
had a holiness to her and she wasn't someone to say no to.

And so, after a long absence, Betty took to attending early
weekday masses, sitting with her rosary among the empty
pews. She knelt and sat and stood in all the right places, with
a small sad smile fixed to her face. But Miss DeCarlo told her
she should be back at the 10.30 mass on a Sunday, back
among her friends.

But they'll all look at me, said Betty. Yes they will, said Miss DeCarlo, especially when you start reading out the bidding prayers. Betty, who could just about bear the thought of skulking unnoticed at the back, was terrified. But already she knew she would take up the suggestion, because old Miss DeCarlo knew what she really needed.

So one Sunday Betty stood up before her old congregation, ashamed and anxious, and read out the words she had typed up the day before. Perhaps there was the odd look, but mostly people just smiled or bowed their heads, too busy thinking about their own things. And Betty, her own public penance fulfilled, saw that the judgement of others was as nothing to her judgement of herself.

The following week, the new parish priest read out another postcard from Father David, who said he was having a wonderful time among his new flock. *The parishioners have given me a really warm welcome,* he wrote, *and my housekeeper can't do enough for me.*

FOODS OF LOVE

We met at a farmer's market, standing by a stall offering South African beef jerky and biodynamic Stilton. I laughed as you hoovered up all the samples, feigning gourmet appreciation to cover your greed.

On our first date, we saw *Super Size Me* at your beloved arthouse cinema, followed by Belgian waffles and ice cream. The next few months were a blur of weekends in bed, fortified by home-made *cafés au lait* and Cumberland sausage sarnies.

The day you proposed, we sat against a windbreak on the beach, one cold February morning. Remember? We shared a tray of vinegary chips to wash down the little bottle of warm Cava you'd bought along. (I've still got the wooden fork somewhere.)

The allotment. Years it took to get it, and then we found chard and squash were about the only things we could grow that didn't get eaten away. But all those wonderful picnics we had there, drinking stewed tea from your grandad's old Thermos. Rummagings in the shed. And all those excruciatingly ingenious marrow recipes . . .

After I gave birth to the twins, you surprised me with a feast of things I'd had to give up while pregnant: bubbly, Brie and prawns. Mealtimes took on their happy routine: slow-cooker casseroles on a Saturday, Sunday roast, hot chocolate after the kids' school concerts, your eccentric 'power salads' in summer.

For your fiftieth, I got you that French Country Cooking course you were always going on about. It was always easier to get you to cook when it was for some birthday or special event – I lacked the 'big match temperament', you'd say. (You lacked the 'washing-up-as-you-go gene', I'd reply.)

And so we entered a double-cream era of *cassoulets* and *tartiflettes, ragoûts* and *terrines de veau, soufflés* and *coq au vin*. You were happy to drive miles for an obscure ingredient or kitchen implement, something you'd only ever use once that was then tucked away in the back of the cupboard with all the other oddities.

After your scare came the keep-fit years – the bikes, the lycra, the couscous, the pine nuts, your obsession with fresh carrot juice. Our Katie marrying Alexios and the big fat Greek wedding feast his family put on – we didn't eat for a week afterwards. Our retirement trip to Japan, and our first (and only) taste of fish sperm and curry doughnuts.

But of all the meals that make up a marriage, I never saw this one on the menu: vending-machine Hula Hoops for me, and nil-by-mouth for you.

THE GREAT WILLIE WHIZZ-BANG!

Kids. I hate kids.

It's almost impossible to find one you can bum a fag off these days. And you have to watch everything you say to them, can't make any decent gags, for risk of causing offence.

The other day I was doing a gig, leading the kids through my limbo disco challenge, and at the side I saw a little toddler sitting on her mum, jiggling up and down in time to 'Oops Upside Your Head'.

'Look at her!' I shouted. 'She's *lap-dancing!*'

The secret of a good kids' entertainer is to have some jokes up your sleeve for the adults too, and this one used to be a *banker*. A couple of the dads did snigger, but afterwards the mum in charge took me to one side. As she handed over the balance of my so-called 'fee', she came over all serious, said thank you for the show but she felt duty-bound to offer some feedback.

'Your cash is the only feedback I need, love – please feel free to give as generously as you like,' I said. But she was one of those buttoned-up Margot types, and this didn't seem to go down very well.

'You really got the children going,' she said at last. 'And that's great.' Of course it's great love, I nearly said, I'm a professional. Twenty-one years I've been at this game, man and boy. Or rather man and older man.

But she wasn't done. Somewhere, buzzing over our heads, there was a big old *But* waiting to dump its load. Finally she spat it out.

'But . . . I just wonder if some of your material is really quite appropriate in this day and age?'

Oh my days. Here we go. Turns out she didn't like the lap-dancing gag. Or the bit where I tricked birthday girl's dad into handing his daughter a tenner. Or when I chased the littl'un round, threatening to kiss her to death. Mum didn't approve of my musical vaping game. She didn't even like my Fu Manchu impression, for God's sake.

'Couldn't that be construed as, er, a tad racist, Mister, er, Whizz-Bang?'

'Please,' I said. 'Call me Jean-Paul.'

'Um, er, Jean-Paul.'

'Only joking, love! Call me Umberto.'

'Er, ah, Umberto.'

'Oh come on, love! Don't you know a Willie when you see one?'

'Willie. Right.'

Gotcha. And *couldn't you be construed as an uptight old fart with a broomstick where your funny bone should be?* I nearly replied. (In fact she was pretty fit, in a ladies-who-lunch-and-do-aquarobics-five-times-a-week sort of way. I mean you probably would. Well I wouldn't. Vi's the only one for me, always has been. And come to think of it now, I *couldn't*.)

But no. The customer is always right, even – or especially – when they're a *right one*. Never queer your pitch, as I always say, even with a queer couple (of whom there are more and more these days, you'd be surprised). Never cut off your red nose to spite your clownface.

I'd heard it all before, of course. Standard fare in a PC world gone mad, alas. A world where all the fun of things has been drowned out by the Health & Safety mafia. But I knew what to say.

Tradition, love, I said. Taste of authentic British working-class humour, I said. Roots in vaudeville bawdy. That essay by George Orwell. She lapped it all up. In fact, by the time I got my lips round *commedia dell'arte*, I wondered if she wasn't rather warming to me.

Just then, the husband came over. He'd obviously been encouraging her to speak her mind, and now he was checking that she'd got everything off her chest. She nodded discreetly, and he switched into charm mode at once.

'Interesting game you're in,' he says to me, in that way that posh people speak when they're trying to sound blokeish. 'How did you come to be a children's entertainer?'

'I got made redundant from the print in the mid-eighties, and sort of fell into it,' I say. 'My wife encouraged me. Said I should put my inner clown to work for us. She came up with the name too – only name in the book with an exclamation mark in it.'

'Westward Ho!?' he says, arching a clever-clever eyebrow.

'Nah,' I say. 'At this hour I'll probably just take the North Circular.' *Gotcha.*

'It's a really fun name,' he says, a trifle miffed.

'Actually, it was my wife's nickname for me already,' I say, and we both stare at the floor for a bit. 'Anyway, the rest is history. Ten thousand kids in stitches since then, and not a bedpan in sight.'

He gives me a sort of sideways look. 'Funny how many words for making people laugh are about violence and murder, isn't it?' he says. 'You know: I had them *in stitches*, I *slayed* them, I really *killed* tonight . . .'

Jeez. Not that old fucking chestnut. I put on my best

Freud accent. 'Achtung Herr Doktor! You're not going to start wiv ze analysis, are you?'

'Actually,' he says, looking almost sheepish all of a sudden. 'I am an analyst.'

'Go on then,' I say. 'Give us a twirl.'

Now *he* puts on the accent. '*Vell, let's just say I vouldn't vant to be there when ze laughter stops.*'

My phone vibrates. It's a text from Vi: *Are you ever coming home? I can't find my phone.*

'Ach, Doktor Feelgood, you are spoiling us,' I say. 'Would you like to know how big my mother's penis was too?'

Don't worry, hun, I text Vi back. *I'll be back in two shakes of a camel's ding-dong.* It's an old joke of ours. She used to like it, though she probably won't remember it now.

She probably won't even remember to check her phone, come to that. After all, she thinks she's lost her phone. She texted me to say so. On her *phone*. But no, another text. *What's all this about a camel? Is everything OK love?*

Right as rain, I text back from the analyst's pot pourri-reeking crapper. *On my way. Traffic's a bit stationery – be with you in a jiffy bag.*

Another old fave. I look down at the toilet bowl to see the now-familiar cloud of red seeping through the old amber nectar.

Ah the wee of a clown, as Smokey nearly said, when there's no one else around.

And I think: *Here's another one you won't get.*

'What's your name, Daphne?'

'Daphne!'

'*Daphne!* Why didn't you say so?'

She's giggling so much she's gone all red in the face. You'd think the kids would tire of their entertainer pretend-ing to forget the name of the birthday girl (or boy), or getting her age wrong by a factor of 1000, but they don't. They really don't.

When I started out, I wanted to get away from all that cliched claptrap, all those '*Oh no it's nots!*' and '*I can't hear yous!*' I even tried to dispense with the bendy wand and the magic colouring book – you know, first the pictures are all black and white, but then – *if we all try really hard, kids* – we can magic all the colour back into the pictures! What? *It didn't work?* Come on then, kids, *let's try one more time . . .*

All that bollocks. No, I thought I'd be radical and different. I introduced some crazy shit, like vegetable telepathy and sci-fi fairy tales (I was especially proud of *Goldilocks and the Three Mutant Cyber Killer-Clowns*).

But I soon knocked all that on the head. Kids are kids. There's no point trying to be new or different with kids. They like the same old silly familiar stuff, and then they like it some more. And ideally, after that, they'd like you to do it all over again.

'Daphne!' I say. 'That was my grandad's name!'

She looks bemused, but the grown-ups like it. This is more my sort of crowd, today. Lots more normal types, lots of grans and grandads, less *Guardian* readers and muesli munchers. Not a Remoaner in sight, by the looks, thank gawd.

I pull out a prize from The Great Willie Whizz-Bang!'s Big Bag of Prizes. (I always spend a good fifteen minutes at the top of the gig going through all the tat the kids can win, so long as they do what they're told, sit still when I ask them to, stay on the right side of the line, and generally obey The Great Willie Whizz-Bang! at all times. As I always say, you're nothing without crowd control in this game.)

'Look Daphne!'

It's a little paratrooper man – a figure with a silk parachute attached. I used to love these when I was a kid. Throw it out the window, watch him catch a breeze and sail down into the yard.

'Here Daphne, would you like this little man as your prize?'

She shakes her head, as I knew she would.

'No?' I say, and I turn to the oldies with a slightly suggest-ive wink. 'You'll *like* soldiers when you're *older*, Daphne!' The grans love it.

I put on the bubble machine and grab the chance of a quick breather. Vi texts: *Have you seen the oven gloves? Need to change the guinea pigs.*

We've never had guinea pigs, love, I want to text back. *And the oven's switched off at the mains now, when I'm not in the house.* It has to be – ever since WaffleGate, alas. We've still got the scorch marks on the ceiling, bless her.

Birthday girl Daphne's back up on stage, inevitably. And now she's pointing at my make-up.

'Why have you got tears painted on your face?'

'Those aren't tears, my love,' I shoot back. 'Those are tattoos. There's one for every Blood I've burned.'

Not everyone got it. But I was on top of my game today, totally *smashed* it. Sometimes I think it's a shame my best material is wasted on the kids. But then I remember: it's saying it in front of the kids that makes it so funny.

Done right, even just saying the words 'gender reassign-ment' or 'colonic irrigation' or 'PET scan' can bring the house down. Just had the results of mine, I tell them. Turns out I'm clear of rabbits, but there's a dark area they want to do more tests on. Doctors think it might be a fur ball. Now I need a CAT scan!!

Actually my chances are pretty good. Anyway, it only hurts when I laugh.

Don't worry love, I text Vi back. *I'll be home in time for* Neighbours. *We've got to keep up with the Joneses!*

Another old chestnut. Obviously *Neighbours* isn't broadcast on the weekend, technically. But Vi likes to think it is, and it's no biggie to keep up the impression. It's one of the few things that calms her down when it all gets too much. First thing, last thing, any time really – just tell her it's time to head for Ramsay Street and you can literally see the anxiety draining out of her.

Not that I blame her for her outbursts. Even if she does punch and kick sometimes.

It's not easy to keep a straight face when you're losing your mind.

I got an email from a parents' association this morning, from some do-gooder from one of the local schools. Asking if I would be interested in performing for half an hour at their summer fair.

Not that they could offer a fee or anything.

'We're sorry we can't offer up-front remuneration in these times of austerity and school cuts,' it said. 'But you will of course have the chance to promote your unique talents to a captive audience of several hundred mums and dads – all of whom have little ones with birthdays that need livening up!'

Laugh? I nearly bought a round. This was the third request to work for free I'd had in a fortnight. And having just taken out another credit card to cover the interest on the others, it caught me at a bad moment.

If you'd been to one of my shows, you'd know I put in lots of preparation and work very hard at my performances, I emailed back. *I don't just dial it in like that Mr MangoTrousers or that Benny BongoBongo* (who I happen to know stole most of his act from a holiday rep in Marbella).

Asking me to perform free is a bit like asking a restaurant to come along and cook for nothing on the off chance that someone might book a dinner with them a few months later, I said.

Mind you, I'd perform for twenty-four hours free in exchange for one decent erection.

*

That's me out of the Kids' Entertainer Guild.

It was a big party for a whole load of different ages, on a big green space round the back of a block of flats. Lots of families had got together to hold a joint bash with bouncy castles, a pool, a big slide, trampolines, the works.

I was only supposed to be gigging for the little ones. But for some reason the older ones thought it'd be fun to crash my show. They jeered my jokes. They pelted me with bananas. They sprayed silly string in my face and they squirted me with their long-range sub-automatic water rifles. Still, at least I had a big finish for them.

Vi had texted a bit earlier: *How do I get out of here?* I texted back: *Where are you?* She replied, *I'm in the café.* Good, I thought. She's worked it out.

So I got the lariest kid of the lot up to help me with a magic trick. Told him I was going to sever his head from his body, but it wouldn't hurt at all.

My phone vibrates. Another message: *Which way is home?*

Up he came, like a lamb to the slaughter. (*Slaughter*, don't forget, Herr Doktor, is just an *s* away from *laughter*.) He laid himself down in my comedy stocks, giggling to his mates all the while. I did a bit of business with a giant pair of plastic scissors, covered him completely in my silken Cape of Magic & Mystery, and subtly moved my right ankle into position.

Now, under cover of the cape, I pulled up my trouser leg, told the kid to close his eyes and open his mouth ... *Who's laughing now?* I say, as I decant the contents of my catheter bag.

Not really. *Gotcha.*

I mean, I like a joke as much as the next man. But I'm a pro. And you've got to keep the laughs up, haven't you? 'Cos when the laughter stops, that's called dying.

AN EFFUSION
OF THE DIVINE FEMININE

'Dave Travis, News Desk.'

'Dave, it's Ben.'

'Ben! Where are you? You're late. Never mind. Doesn't matter. Listen, when you get in, can you make a start on the News in Briefs, tidy up the page two splash, then give Stan's leader on post-Brexit economics the once-over? Usual problem – it's a thing of erudition and grace, of course, but I've a nasty feeling it's also a load of old bollocky tosh-wank too.'

'I won't be in today, Dave.'

'Very funny. And after that, can you give—'

'I'm sorry Dave. I just can't be there today.'

'You what?'

'Something happened last night. Well, early this morning actually.'

'Oh I get it. You stayed on at the Three Compasses for the lock-in, and now you feel odd.'

'Like I've never felt before.'

'Ah, got one of those existential hangovers, have we? Panicky, anxious, tearful? Don't worry about it, Ben, happens to the best of us. To you more than most, admittedly, but—'

'It's not that. It's . . .'

'Oh come on, Ben! Just neck some coffee, have a shower, bang one out, carrot juice and ginger, hair of the dog, three raw eggs and a teaspoon of paprika . . . whatever your patent remedy is, just sort yourself out and get in here as soon as you can. Tony's got the face on already.'

'Camomile tea.'

'Eh?'

'Nothing. I'm just not sure anything will ever be the same again, actually, Dave.'

'Oh God, bit of substance abuse, was there, Ben? Not utterly advisable on a school night when we go to press the following morning, but never mind. Good for you, Ben. You're a hack, you overdid it, comes with the job description. Now just get your shit together and get in here. Please. *I'm fucking drowning here.*'

'I'm sorry Dave. I really can't. Something happened . . . Or perhaps *someone.*'

'Oh God no, Ben. Please.'

'It's not like that, Dave.'

'It never is, with you. Look, I'm sure she's amazing. Why don't you come in and we can chat all about it . . . while you're doing some actual work? That way you can tell me about your future wife and I can hang on to my existing one by not getting fired?'

'It's not a physical thing, Dave.'

'Oh dear Lord. You are such a cliché.'

'DAVE WILL YOU JUST LET ME TRY AND SPEAK MY TRUTH? I'm trying to tell you about something that could change your whole life, like it has mine.'

Pause. 'OK, let's hear it.'

'Well, about 4am, I woke up suddenly with a very strange sensation.'

'Were your underpants on back to front?'

'Listen. Please. I suddenly felt . . . with the utmost certainty . . . that there was someone in my room. A presence. And yet . . . not a harmful one.'

'Come again?'

'Suddenly the room went very dark and then just as suddenly very light, as if illumined from within by a sort of benevolent pinkish glow. I felt an intense burning in the back of my neck. I was moved to roll out of bed and onto my knees. Then a voice within me said, very distinctly: "Now you shall live in the light of my love."'

'Ben, I . . . Proceed.'

'I looked up in the corner of my room, and saw a face smiling at me. But not like any other face you've ever seen, Dave. An expression of infinite pity and piety and kindness. A countenance of all-knowing purity and forgiveness. A . . .'

'Just a face, you say?'

'Not sure.'

'No hair?'

'Well, it was more an impression than a sharp image.'

'And no *body*?'

'Not this time.'

'This time?'

'There's every likelihood she'll come again tonight.'

'What? She? How?'

'Wait. This is all very new to me too, but I googled my experience and—'

'*You googled your experience?*'

'Yes. I googled my experience.'

'And?'

'And I have every reason to believe that what I experienced last night was . . . *an effusion of the divine feminine.* Possibly a Marian apparition.'

'Marion who?'

'Marian, as in "pertaining to Our Lady".'

'Wait, wait. So you're saying you can't come in to work because the Virgin Mary appeared to you in a vision last night.'

'Early this morning actually. Afterwards I felt the most extraordinary sense of peace and security. I realised that all my worries and anxieties are as nothing when you are held in the loving heart of the Holy Mother.'

'—'

'And that means that I am now free to share her love and be an agent for her vision of unconditional forgiveness, which alone can heal the terrible conflicts and tensions that are tearing this sinful world of ours apart.'

'So . . .'

'So I can't come in today, Dave, because my heart has undergone a radical transformation, and I have pledged henceforth to dedicate what remains of my insignificant earthbound existence to committing only such acts as will contribute to the healing of the world's aching, damaged soul – to the glory of the divine, all-loving matriarch!'

'It would massively heal *my* damaged soul, Ben, if you could get in here and edit a bit of copy this morning.'

'Dave! I haven't even told you the best part yet. There were no flowers in the flat anywhere, and yet after the vision subsided, my flat was filled with a delicate odour of roses.'

'Now *that* is a miracle. I've been in your flat.'

'The rose, in case you don't know, is one of Mary's symbols.'

'I did not know that. I had her down as a tulip girl.'

'Dave. It's easy to mock, I know. But now I see that the cynicism of our profession is just a shield.'

'A shield, Ben?'

'That's right, Dave. The ego doesn't want us to open our hearts and souls to the loving will of the divine because it naturally feels threatened for its own survival. And so it hides behind jokes and mockery in an effort to distract you from the truth. But that's OK.'

'That's OK, Ben?'

'Of course. Fear is only the servant of love. And life will keep presenting you with opportunities to love, until you're ready to take one.'

'Right, right . . . Did the lady have any message for you, Ben? Anything about the importance of hitting deadlines or honouring your employment contract, for instance?'

'I am no longer of that world, Dave. And nor are you, if you could but see it.'

'—'

'Why don't you come round tonight and we'll adore Her together, Dave? No wait, I think veneration is the right term, actually.'

'You venerate her for me, Ben. I have to go now. I think I've just had a vision of my own.'

'What?'

'Most odd.'

'What?'

'Yes, yes. It was Tony, but not as I've ever seen him before. He was kneeling before a statue, as if in prayer.'

'That's incredible! Something is happening here, Dave! This is like Pentecost all over again!'

'Yes! He was muttering something.'

'What was it? Was he speaking in tongues?'

'He was saying something like: *Dear Lord, grant me the wisdom to decide what to do with these two here bollocks of Ben which I have just removed with a machete.*'

'Look, Dave. I can see that you're in a state of spiritual distress. So because you are my *Brother-in-the-Mother*, I'll come in and help out with Press Day just one more time.'

'Thanks Ben.'

'Obviously things'll have to be a little different though.'

'How so?'

'Well I'll be saying the rosary on the hour, every hour. And it'd be nice if you and the rest of the team could join me.'

'Right. Well, we can but ask.'

'Great! See you in about half an hour then. If you still recognise me, that is.'

'How do you mean?'

'Well, obviously I'll be swathed in my Robe of Golden Righteousness.'

'Sounds lovely, Ben. Look if you can dodge Tony on the way in, I'll tell him I asked you to attend that post-Budget Treasury Briefing first thing? It's probably nothing, but sometimes they use those calls to bury a dodgy number or two . . .'

'Thanks Dave, old boy. Shall I grab you a cappuccino on the way in?'

'Oooh yes please. And an almond croissant if there's one left.'

'And if not?'

'Dunno. Any pastry-led comestible, I guess, so long as it's not sultana-facing.'

'Say no more, chief.'

'Ben?'

'Yes?'

'What was the Divine Mother like anyway?'

'Surprisingly good kisser actually.'

BURY ME WITH THE ANIMALS

Inside the entrance hut there were glass cases full of crudely carved farm animals and little ceramic dogs arranged in neat rows. There were photos of some of the centre's best-loved residents down the years – a brood of baby hedgehogs, a tame badger, a heron called Gretchen with a mangled wing. There were displays of birds' nests and snake skins and egg shells and a stuffed badger. The whole place exuded a musty, bird's-nesty sort of smell too.

On one wall there was a display of photos of the animal centre's founder, Karen, receiving recognition for her work: an official opening with the town mayor, a thank you letter from a school for *a lovely visit*, a signed photo from Terry Nutkins. And, in pride of place, a photo of Karen all dressed up at the Palace to receive her gong.

Joe wanted to get the ceramic dogs out. He couldn't, of course – they were a 'collection on kind loan from a supporter', according to a sign. Adult toys, thought Ann to herself, a tricky concept for her three-and-a-half year-old grandson. Joe already knew the answer would be no – he asked every time – and made his request in a plaintive, pre-defeated tone. But this disappointment would soon be forgotten, Ann knew, once they got inside.

Joe loved all the animals (except the goat and the sheepie), knew all their names, knew where they hid in their cages. Harry, Ann's husband, had loved it all too – the ramshackle, amateurish vibe, the army of tireless volunteers undaunted by the crumbling facilities or the overwhelming need, the sense of a single-minded passion taken to the lengths of eccentricity. He had loved coming here with Joe and his other grandkids almost more than the children did.

Ann was delighted that Joe enjoyed it here so much too. But privately, she found the place tatty and smelly, and the emphasis on animal life over human a bit obsessive. She'd seen a rat in here once.

At the till where you paid to go in, a fidgety woman with permanent eye-liner was holding out a hessian bag. 'I've got a bat in here,' she said. 'Found it just lying behind the garage door. It's breathing but it won't move.' She held the bag open so Ann could lift Joe up to peer in at the tiny dark lump of membrane and skin.

The cashier nervously called out over the walkie-talkie. At last Karen herself appeared.

'What is it?' said the woman with the bat in a bag.

'It's a pipistrelle,' said Karen.

'*What's that?*' said the woman with disgust.

'That's the *breed.* Look, I won't mess around with it here, I'll get it inside where we can do a proper check.'

Talk about variety in your work, mused Ann. One day you get a pony that's been left abandoned on the roadside, next day you get a parakeet that's fallen out of its tree. And now she's got a bat.

The woman who'd brought the bat didn't want Karen to go. There was something she needed to ask.

'Does that mean someone I know is going to die?'

'No,' said Karen. 'Who told you that?'

'My neighbour. She said it happened to her. She said she found a dead bat on her kitchen roof and next day she got a call to say her mother-in-law had died.'

'*Don't you ever listen to such things,*' said Karen fiercely.

Just inside the entrance, there was an old boat that had been turned into a flower bed, a jolly jumble of hollyhocks, nasturtiums, jasmine and pansies. Harry had taken a picture of this once with his phone, and had used the image for the screen-saver on their PC in the living room. Until she'd discreetly swapped it for one of the grandchildren, that is – Vicky, Paula and Joe, taken at Whipsnade on Paula's sixth birthday. Joe would have still been three then and Vicky nine.

It was the last time they'd all been together – she and Harry, their daughter Chrissy, the little ones. Well, not counting Guy, whom nobody would have seen for six years come Christmas. In the one letter he'd written in all that time, he said he'd regretfully decided to 'deconnect from Family and other inherited patterns'. He could no longer see people who were 'undermining my positivity' and 'blocking the vital work of attaining universal oneness'. *Bloody brain-washers.*

She'd never shown the letter to Harry. She didn't think he'd have been strong enough to take it. He'd always been funny about his son, about what he owed him as his father. Harry had always dipped in and out of Chrissy's life, and she'd always stroked and indulged and forgiven her dad, whatever he did or didn't do. But with Guy, Harry seemed to take his parental responsibilities very literally.

Harry always tried to *be there* for Guy. He'd take time off work to attend Guy's first-team football games, concerts and school assemblies, and even taught himself how to cast so he could take his son night-fishing. He played the role of the attentive dad, but there was always a dutiful quality to what he did; somehow it didn't come across as natural, as *felt.*

Somewhere along the line, it seemed to her now, Guy had picked up on this and had basically just – what was that phrase? – *consciously uncoupled* from Harry. Just went off him, found substitute father figures everywhere – a teacher at school, an older colleague at his first job after uni whom they'd initially had their suspicions about (actually he was a nice enough old stick, just a lonely widower looking for a companion he could lecture on mineralogy). And now of course David, his 'transformation facilitator'. (Wretched cultists.)

Ann opened the gate, and Joe ran on ahead as always. He was safely off the leash in here, in this zoo-cum-open-air ward full of traumatised geese, blind hedgehogs, lame ferrets and one overly tame fallow deer.

On the right there was a cage with a squirrel in. Often there were lots of other squirrels round here too, scampering over the wire and staring in at their incarcerated compatriot. This always tickled Harry. 'They're asking him: *Here, what you in for??*' he'd say. It wasn't a bad joke, not the first time anyway.

The main enclosure was a grassy, fenced-in square that contained hens and India runner ducks and a few static goats with curly horns. A newish addition was a rough-looking sheep called Julie. Julie's matted wool was thick and pendulous, apart from some sore-looking bald patches.

Joe *really did not like* this sheep. She would come right up to the fence, fix you with her satanic yellow eyes, and make a deep, metallic *baa* right at you, over and over again. This wasn't a sheep that was hungry or in need of attention. This was a sheep that was spoiling for a fight.

Over the way from Julie, a black longhorn goat called Butch had a paddock to himself. A sign informed visitors that

Butch was kept separate from the rest of the animals because he was too aggressive. Joe *really did not like* this goat either.

Sometimes Julie and Butch would bleat menacingly across the way to each other for the whole of a visit. When he had to get past either of these angry herbivores, Joe would cling to his granny's thigh and edge away as fast as he could. Though he'd always ask to come here if given the choice of an outing, his report afterwards was unvarying.

'Did you go to the animals today, Joe?' Harry would ask.

'*We don't like the sheepie.*'

'Did you see the hedgehogs?'

'*We don't like the goat.*'

He'd recite these lines like incantations, even in advance:

'Where shall we go today, Joe?'

'Let's go to the animals, grandma! *But we don't like the sheepie . . .*'

Harry had been tickled by the consistency of Joe's reaction. He even made a song out of it:

Oh we don't like the goat or the sheepie!
We find them really rather creepy . . .

Joe ran on ahead again. The corner with the parakeets and Fred the ferret (usually a no-show) and various random outposts of poultry didn't grab him much. In the cage with the pheasants, he only really liked the cartoonish parrot statue. To Joe, brought up on Disney films and picture books, this statue was more like what a bird should look like than the real ones.

Then there was a pig called Ginny who had grown so corpulent she could barely support her own weight. Ginny was an animal bred for slaughter who had somehow found her way here, to an abattoir-free retirement. (Every animal had its own back-story, of course, usually tragic: abandonment by travellers, a wing caught in the plastic from a four-pack of lager, a hit and run . . .)

'This is unknown territory,' Karen had explained to Harry one time. 'We don't know what happens to these animals when they get this big and old. They've normally all been killed and eaten way before now.' Some days Ginny seemed to manage, waddling about unaided; other times she just lay sprawled out where she had last flopped down after feeding.

'Did you know pigs can get sunburn?' said a hand-scrawled sign. Ann looked at Ginny's obscene, near-bald skin. She thought of pigs with sunburn and of hairy crackling, and felt a bit nauseous.

'Bury me, oh bury me with the animals!' Harry would pronounce at some point on every visit, usually about now, as they stood over this vast beached pig. She hadn't, of course, she'd buried him in Oakford cemetery, alongside his grand-parents and his great-grandparents.

On weekends, when they were old enough to ride a bike, Harry used to like taking the children – and later their grandchildren – over to the graves at Oakford to 'say hello to my mum and dad'. It was a regular weekend thing for him, something he'd obviously grown up with and which brought him the warm familiarity of tradition and continuity.

It had always seemed an odd practice to Ann, she who felt her parents with her all the time. Almost any event or activity could trigger a memory for Ann, from making jam or smell-ing lavender (mum) to seeing an allotment or an Arsenal top (dad). She often pictured her own life as a shape that sat within the outline of theirs, like a smaller lace doily laid over a bigger one, or one cake cutter nested inside another. She had never sought to exceed the boundaries set by her parents; with all the sacrifices they had made for her, it would have been unseemly, disloyal.

The children, anyway, didn't think Harry's cemetery trips morbid – it was a chance for a good bike ride, and there was a decent playground at the end of it. And besides, the cemetery was endlessly fascinating, with its dramatic statuary of guardian angels and crucified near-naked men; the elegant old iron watering cans with their long spouts; and the half-sunken plots that would surely drop them straight to hell if stepped on.

Above all, they loved the green marble-like stones that topped many of the graves – crystalline nuggets the colour of a British sea, which they all took to be some kind of precious treasure and never failed to smuggle home by the pocketful.

Recently, now that that he was buried there too, Ann had gone a couple of times to 'see Harry' in the cemetery herself. But the visits only made her feel more alone. Something real yet unreachable of him was there, and somehow this something was worse than nothing. *Nothing*, after all, was what she had to get used to.

After Ginny came a pair of Jacobs sheep with absurdly curly horns – proper Biblical beasts, Ann always thought, feeling again that tiny twinge of disappointment that Joe never gave them their due. But alas, they were only an adult's idea of the perfect animal to fascinate a child. Joe ran on instead to the next enclosure, where a gaggle of scruffy ducks and geese pecked at each other's feathers or speed-billed discoloured water from a moulded-plastic pond. Their wings were stunted and bedraggled, long bare quills protruding at random angles like the spokes of a broken umbrella.

One white duck, otherwise normal-looking, was doing an endless somersault in the dirty water, head over tail, again and again. Sometimes the hurt is on the inside, thought Ann.

What Joe really liked here were the terrapins – or *frogs* as he called them. They came in small, medium and large versions, their dark slimy extremities edged with pinstripes of bright yellow or orange, like fancy gymwear.

Some days the terrapins were all submerged, and Joe would stare forlorn for ages in the hopes of sighting a penile head breaking the surface or the moving shadow of a shell just below the waterline. Other days they were all lined up for inspection on the pond's brick edge, battle-ready craft set to scramble on the instant. Behind them Brian the new heron stalked up and down with ostentatious sarcasm.

Nothing. And yet. Looking back on their last years together, Ann wondered if the separation process hadn't begun long before Harry died. They had been companionable, she liked to think, but in practice this meant each of them doing their own thing in a different room of an echoing five-bedroomed house. She would be doing her embroidery or glass-painting, or pottering about in the garden; he would be on the PC selling things on eBay, or failing to finish yet another of his books about the Nazis.

People seemed to see them as one of the good couples, one of the happy few whose marriage had survived and thrived through all the years. 'Mum and Dad are still just as cute together as ever,' her daughter Chrissy had said in that lovely speech on the occasion of their thirtieth anniversary. (No Guy, of course, not even for that.)

Certainly Harry knew how to rise to an occasion. He stood up and gave one of his witty replies, making ironic gags about marital violence in a way that everyone assumed masked deep affection he could express no other way. 'Ann would have murdered me years ago,' he said. 'Only she needs me for the weeding . . .' He delighted everyone with his ballroom dancing skills and his soft-shoe shuffles, moving with surprising daintiness for such a big man to the tune of Good Ol' Wally's Mesmerisin' Ragtime Band. (Wally being his old mate Walter Constant from the London office, of course.)

It wasn't as if, behind the curtains, things were toxic. There were no dark scenes of abuse or rage. It was just that, as they got older, they seemed to talk less and less. With their nest empty and both semi-retired, they had each retreated wordlessly to the haven of their respective pastimes. They moved around and about each other with practised ease, like terrapins in a pond.

Now Joe led them down what Ann called Owl Alley, a pathway between two rows of cages containing several kinds of owl, a falcon ('please note this bird was an unwanted pet'), a battered pheasant and a couple of crows.

Harry used to love the crows. He would stand with his head resting on the wooden cross-piece of their enclosure and make that odd squelchy-raspy noise which, in thirty-two years of marriage, she had never heard him make at any other time. She fancied that if she had never come with him to this place, she would never to her dying day (or his) have known he was capable of such a sound. She wondered: did he have other noises for other circumstances that she would never know about?

Once, on holiday, in that brief early window before children, she remembered waking in their little rented cottage to find the space beside her empty. Walking blearily into the kitchen, she found him sitting outside the back door on a white plastic patio chair. He was offering bits of bread and cheese to a crow, whispering softly to the shiny black creature as it hopped through that familiar ritual of human-animal interaction in which fear dances with greed.

He didn't see her, but every day of that holiday he repeated the ritual, and every day the crow inched a bit nearer, shed a bit more fear, gained a little more trust. She took to waking each morning that week, pleasantly muzzy and caffeine-ready, and sneaking downstairs to watch him from the little circular window in the loo. If he knew she was there, he never said anything.

On their very last morning, he succeeded in getting the bird to actually eat out of his hand. Looking to share his triumph, he had turned round to see Ann watching from her little vantage-point. He wore a face of childlike joy she didn't think she'd ever seen before. Unable to reconfigure her own expression in time, she had instinctively started shaking her head at him in mock derision: *soppy man, dirty bird.* And he had quickly turned away, eyes cast down as if caught in a moment of shameless self-pleasure.

Harry could be infuriatingly clipped and turned in on himself when he wanted to be, especially in later years, but it seemed there was a streak of tenderness in him so tender he could only safely share it with animals.

She had hated herself for sending that moment away. And she hated that he had never offered her another one.

Harry had made a few bids for a cat or a puppy in the early years of their marriage, especially when initiated by Guy. But Ann, with her unimpeachable domestic pre-eminence, had easily shot them down. Pets were dirty and smelly and messy, she said; they brought other little creatures with them and *it'll be me who ends up having to do all the clearing up.* But now she wondered how their life might have been different with a golden retriever to retire with, say, or a couple of cats.

Just as couples thinking about having a baby often start by rehearsing the rigours of parental self-sacrifice on a pet, so couples she knew whose children had left home often turned again to an animal – another 'child' to worry about and fuss over, a new warm and endearing little body to project a personality onto.

Something to fill the holes of a very approximate marriage of hearts and minds.

He had died on a train. On the way to work. Two stations in to his daily commute to Waterloo, the heart attack had swamped him. Down Harry went, down among the discarded crisp packets and the muddy boot marks. Down and dead on a dirty, smelly train. One fall, one submission.

It was Chrissy who had broken the news to her. Ann had been round at her sister's, and Chrissy had driven over. 'This is a nice surprise!' she'd said, like a fool, and Chrissy had given her a weird twisted smile. Hadn't known what to do with her face, poor thing.

Ann's first thought was to try and phone Guy. Even at the time, she'd known it was an excuse to contact her son. But he couldn't come to the phone, they said. He was leading a Channelling Retreat and the group's healing energy seal couldn't be broken. '*I'll break your energy seal in a minute!*' she'd retorted. She never heard from him again.

Two children – a daughter who's sorted, a son lost to a cult. But three lovely grandchildren and a marriage worth missing, on balance. Perhaps it wasn't such a bad tally.

In the animal centre's memorial garden, in among the statues of St Francis and the stone bird baths, there were memorial messages from pet owners to their beloved deceased animals – plaques to affectionate Yorkies and faithful Labs, heartfelt dedications to mischievous rabbits and playful Siamese cats, a cross marking the grave of 'a fox and friend to us all'.

And there at last was the sign she'd been looking for, the one she'd drafted (Karen hadn't been happy with the wording at first, but an extra donation had soon sorted that):

IN MEMORY OF HARRY

MUCH-LOVED HUSBAND, DAD AND GRANDAD, AND

LOVER OF ALL THE ANIMALS HERE

(EXCEPT THE GOAT AND THE SHEEPIE)

INFINITE RAINBOWS

People sometimes asked Rick if he travelled for his work. It was a question he kept meaning to tuck away for use at the next barbecue with the neighbours, when he always struggled to come up with new small-talk prompts that he hadn't used at the previous barbecue.

Yes, I do actually, thought Rick. Last week I was in Doncaster and Reading. The week before it was Slough and Swindon. I'm also often in Glasgow, Bromley and Hull. Rick travelled to clients and prospects, criss-crossing the country to lead workshops and support on pitches, to attend tissue meetings and wash-ups and beauty parades and blamestorms. As a result of all this, he spent a lot of time in trains, and had come to some fixed conclusions about London stations.

He was dutifully tolerant of Victoria and its eternal building works, as one might be of an elderly mother, since it was the London station of his childhood. He was as stupidly charmed as any tourist by the faux village set-up of Marylebone. He was warily amused by Liverpool Street, with its City sass and vim, like a dad with a boisterous teenage daughter who is on the verge of eluding him forever. He was bored by Waterloo, wilfully under-impressed by the new Kings Cross, but quietly amorous of bohemian St Pancras, with her pianos and her clandestine continental connections. He was intrigued by Fenchurch Street, station of mystery, since he had never been there.

But Paddington, brash and expansive and unhelpful, oppressed him. With its perverse signposting, its absence of sightlines, its long walks between connections, its barriers at the wrong end of platforms, its sinister ability to appear in two different places on the tube map – with its refusal, in short, to act like a proper station, *Paddington could fuck right off.*

At the café where he chose to wait for his train, queue-forming protocols had become ambiguous. A pair of bridge-and-tunnel types – two middle-aged women with silk scarves and floral luggage – stood at right angles to Rick by the counter. They had clearly got there first, but to the untrained eye it might have seemed as if they had already been served, or as if Rick was trying to get in ahead of them. One of the women flashed Rick a look of such scandalised hatred that he fell in love with her at once. He flashed back a smile of exaggerated obeisance – offering a comedy medieval mime to indicate his deference to her and her friend's advanced queue status and nobly refraining from pointing out their eccentric positioning, which to his mind had caused all the trouble in the first place – and began plotting ways to kill them with kindness.

But no. He would not go there; he was stressed enough about the day's workshop already.

He took a deep breath. It was easy to forget that there were people who travelled by rail for the fun of it. On inter-city trains in the daytime, after all, the world of work ruled supreme. People marked their table-top territories with the full panoply of laptops and headphones, expensive travel mugs and stationery porn. As Rick walked through the carriages, he saw people casually parsing Rosetta-stone spreadsheets, constructing lengthy passive-aggressive emails with highly politicised uses of cc-ing and bcc-ing, compiling turgid slidedecks in which the projected figures for the next Q are always somehow trending up.

And above all he heard them, braying and wheedling and bossplaining on their phones, as they dressed down junior team members, sold toasters by the thousand, discussed their chances of winning seven-figure contracts, and snarked at their agencies in heated conference calls. ('Has Carrie actually signed off on this iteration, Jay? The user experience is about as far away from elegant simplicity as it could be, it really is.') And they did it all with unselfconscious ostentation, Rick noted, often involving the whole carriage in their drama.

He was wearing a new shirt. Out of the packet, it transpired to be so blindingly white and starched and sharply creased as to appear the very opposite of smart – like crap fancy dress, in fact. (He remembered randomly that he was still someone who didn't know what 'diffident' meant.)

There was a lot riding on the workshop with today's client, a leading global provider of something something investment solutions. They reportedly had a big budget, and an appetite to do lots more if today went well – but also, at the same time, a cheerful acceptance that if nothing got done for a very long time, that didn't really matter either. They didn't have a clue, as far as he could see, and they were utterly unaware that Rick didn't have a clue. They should, in short, have been the ideal client.

Except that, rather than wallow in blissful ignorance, the client had been led to believe (not least by Rick, alas) that he and his company had the knowhow to lead them out of the wilderness. They kept deferring to his judgement, terrorising him with their childlike faith in his abilities. Rick had clearly talked far too good a game at the pitch, because here he was now, trapped in a room with a load of Senior Global Something Somethings, all of whom expected to be dazzled by the strategic brilliance of a man who had never understood what 'strategy' actually meant.

Rick wondered, and not for the first time: Do other people really approach these meetings thinking, 'I am a powerful agent of transformation!' and 'Today I will be mostly smashing it!' and 'Time to board the Change-Train, people!' Rather than, say: 'Do we have to do this?' or 'Can't this all please go away?' or 'Would you mind counting me out?' or 'Wish I was dead'? (Asking for a friend.)

The warm-up hadn't gone too badly, at least. Rick got everyone to go around and share a fact about themselves that no one else in the room knew. One woman had once shared a taxi with David Beckham, another was a secret crochet fan; the Head of Digital Something revealed that he had never tried Weetabix.

They were not long into the meeting proper before an unspoken consensus emerged that the pet phrase of the gathering would be 'To your point.' Every workshop has a pet phrase, Rick believed, and this one was good enough to add to his elite store of meeting staples. It was right up there with 'What does everyone else think?' and 'Shall we take that one offline?' and 'That's not a sentence I expected to hear today!'

Beginning your remarks with 'to your point' flattered the addressee that you thought their comment had been worth returning to and developing. It convinced the person who said it that they were a master of logic and joined-up thinking. And it flattered everyone by making it seem that the meeting was not just another cosmetic rehearsal of stale platitudes, but was instead a lively and creative symposium in which the powerful thoughts of great minds could be seen to develop and progress towards important, actionable conclusions.

But on top of all that, the very greatest thing about 'to your point' was that different people's contributions didn't need to connect together in any way at all:

'I'm not sure if we know enough yet about who our clients are, or what their true commercial drivers are.'

'To your point . . . I really wish we'd stop using that teal colour for the background on our Twitter quote cards. I know it's in the new brand palette, but it just looks a bit lurid to me.'

After lunch Rick began again with another mini warm-up. He got everyone to say whether they preferred *Breaking Bad* or *Game of Thrones*, and to give reasons for their choice. All was going swimmingly till they got round to the Chief Something Officer, who insisted that she had never watched either and would rather talk about *Mad Men* instead. Rick the mild-mannered socialist fumed. *Honestly*, he thought. *It's one rule for them and one for everyone else . . .*

While Rick toiled with his meagre tools of war – his slides and his whiteboard markers and his blue-tacked flipchart sheets – he noticed that an entire aspirational lifestyle was popping up outside his client's window. It was a Friday afternoon, and for some the weekend was beginning early. Bars spilled out onto terraces, and the balconies of loft-style apartments were suddenly full of loafing urbanites supping chilled prosecco as they gazed out over the children splashing with loud pleasure in the fountain of a bright new public square. The fountain boasted a sheer-flowing water feature whose metallic planes glinted infinite rainbows in the swoon and sheen of the afternoon's unexpected sunburst. Paddling barefoot, a pair of young lovers kissed for the first time.

Around the square, slogans asked: 'What are you thinking right now?' and 'What if you just took a moment?' and 'Isn't life amazing?!' A sign flashed up: 'Giggle. Wonder. *Breathe.*' In one corner, a police horse stood magnificently still, preening with proud muscularity as its officer brushed and stroked and sluiced it down. A small crowd of appreciative children and mums had gathered to enjoy this blessèd moment.

Back in the room, the Post-It notes were wilting in the heat and dropping from the walls. Rick's deck had got stuck on a slide which said only, 'Strategy: Why → How'. It was a slide Rick had devised in a moment of insight many moons ago, but which now blinked back at him, blank and surly.

The sun beat into the room unpleasantly. Rick reflected that if he had set out to wear a scratchy, starchy shirt designed for the express purpose of showing up the starkest possible contrast between the non-sweaty and the now all-too-sweaty areas of his body, areas which of course spread out from under his arms but also now included a growing patch in his upper middle chest area plus, he could confidently surmise, a linear vertical stripe running down the centre of his back . . . well, this would have been that shirt.

No matter. One of the assembled clients – the Assistant Something Account Something – was now enjoying his sixth or seventh epiphany of the hour.

'So I guess what you're saying is that, essentially, in a sense, our strategy should, in a way, be, kind of, *no-strategy*?' It was the young, eager one, the one who always tried too hard. He had got Rick out of several tight spots already that afternoon, because although he wouldn't shut up and had no idea what he was saying, the rest of the group felt obliged to respect his input, even though the conversation had digressed and even regressed on several occasions thanks to him already.

'To your point, that could be *exactly* what I'm saying,' said Rick. Was he? He certainly liked the idea of the follow-up work from the workshop involving the development of a non-strategy. But just then his highly-attuned client sensors picked up a micro-grimace from a more senior stakeholder.

'Or not?' he added, hastily. 'What does everyone think?'

It had turned into another classic flop-chart presentation*. But thankfully it was too late and too hot for anyone to care.

As he was making his way through the client's security gate afterwards, Rick compiled a quick obituary of himself. *He was a man who was born, assembled some garden furniture, and then – to your point – died.*

In his bag, he still had the birthday card from his 45th. They were studiously low-key about birthdays in his office, and his had fallen on a weekend that year. He'd come in to find a card on his desk, and decided to see how long he could go without opening it. All day as it turned out; no one mentioned it at all. When eventually he did look, not long before home time, it was to discover that only three people had signed it. Out of spite, he deleted his comedy all-department thank-you email about how he was adjusting to hitting the big three-oh.

After a much-delayed journey home, during which he had to deal with three heated calls, a provocative text and six pointed emails from his boss, Rick arrived back in London to discover that Paddington was still there.

Next morning, at breakfast, he was taciturn and morose. His mind teetered helplessly on the hair-trigger of irritability. The children ignored him.

'I don't know why you bother to join us for these meals,' said Lorna. 'It's obvious you'd rather be somewhere else.'

I can choose how to respond to this situation, thought Rick. It's entirely within my power. I can be aggressive if I choose . . . Or I can be passive-aggressive.

He looked up, suddenly inspired. 'Now that's not a sentence I expected to hear today!' he said. 'What does everyone else think?'

---

* **Flop-chart presentation:** A presentation using pretty graphs and fancy animations to mask an absence of any real ideas or useful information.

YOU'VE GOT
A HOLD ON ME

I do always try to dine out with my management team once a quarter, just so they know that I'm watching their backs and that my door is always open. It's a chance for them to get to know the real me a little more, meet Toby, glimpse the hinterland behind the commercial firebrand. And of course I need to know if any of them are showing any signs of jumping ship or otherwise *fucking me over*.

If I was dreading this dinner, you can imagine what Toby thought about it. Once he'd even remembered it was happening at all, of course – or that he'd promised to put in an appearance.

With the hubster, I would have to draw on all my client engagement and persuasive sales skills. I was going to have to really twist his arm.

'I want them to get to know the real person behind the high performer,' I said, as I bent it behind his back.

'What on earth for?' he scoffed, dodging my attempted shoulder claw. 'Isn't it bad enough that you have to work with these people? I never expect you to turn up and romance my colleagues, so fuck knows why you think I should want to meet yours.'

'I'd love nothing more than to get to know your col-leagues, as you well know,' I said, following up with a reverse chin-lock. 'You've never once asked.'

'I wouldn't dream of inflicting them on you.'

'Couldn't you at least join us for drinks before dinner, love? You said you were in town today anyway. Laurent's going to join us too. You know, the one you secretly lust over.'

'I don't!' He paused.

He bloody does. I mean, we all do.

'All right,' he said at last, as I moved him seamlessly from a three-quarter face lock to a camel clutch. 'I'll come. Only, you know.'

'What?'

'Nothing.'

'What?'

'Nothing.'

'Come on. *Don't do this*, Toby.' I had him in a half-cobra now.

'Just . . . don't do that thing you do.'

'What thing?'

'The thing where you suck all the attention out of the room.'

'I don't know what you mean.'

'Yes you do. Where you go all Alan Cumming on us all and you have to be the centre of everything and you tell stories and anecdotes and rope people in to agree with you, and laugh at the so-called punchlines even before you've deliv-ered them, and everyone knows them anyway . . .'

'I'm a high-energy person! And *thank God*. If it was left to you, we'd have all mulched to death years ago.'

'What's that supposed to mean?' He'd swivelled with surprising speed and now had me in a crippler crossface, the bastard.

'You're so downbeat. You sit there with the weight of the world on your shoulders. Finding the cloud to every silver lining. Face like a slapped arse. Making it clear you'd rather be anywhere else but here.' Ambitious, but I moved in for a standing head-scissors . . .

'Now hang on. You're the one who holds everyone to ransom with your mood. I look at your face, I know exactly what kind of evening I'm going to have.' He dodged me with a practised sidestep and reverted to the cross-lock.

'Maybe you ought to have the strength of character to define your own evening.'

'Oh I can. But you are like a conversational *black hole*. You enter a room and it's palpable – that desperate hunger for attention. That pathological need. I can feel it burning into me with my back turned.'

Ouch. I was not expecting that stepover toehold face-lock.

'At least I sing for my supper. While you sit there and subtly undercut everything I'm doing or saying.'

'That's just badinage. For contrast.'

'Contrast my arse. You have quite the little negative charisma yourself.'

'You are a card-carrying narcissist.'

'And you are a miserable shit.'

'So . . . Edinburgh Food Studio for 7.30pm?' With my semi-inverted Indian headlock I had him, and he knew it.

'Make it eight.'

Sigh. I sometimes think WWE is the only thing we have in common these days.

THE PATHS OF THE GREAT
LOVERS CROSS
AT VICTORIA STATION

Really, what were the chances? He was on his way to a meeting with a recruitment agency in the area; she was there to catch a Gatwick Express to the airport, whence she would be flying back to Brazil after a week visiting friends in London. The idea that their paths should cross at that very moment, after all this time . . . frankly, it beggared belief.

It had been more than thirty-one years since they'd last seen each other, since she'd waved him off at the airport in Rio. *He had to go home to complete his training, but he'd be back after that and then they'd get engaged,* he said. *Or you could come to London and get a job there?*

Neither of these things would ever happen, she suspected. The relationship hadn't been working for a while. His easygoing, laid-back charm – so different from the men she'd known before him – had turned out on closer inspection to be a craven, jealous passivity. *He* thought she was becoming distant because she was seeing someone else. But he never knew, and she herself only half-understood, that she was slipping into a severe depression.

And yet, they had been Great Lovers, hadn't they? He remembered it all as if it was yesterday. When they'd met, back when he was still a student, they had been *obsessed* with each other. Their love lit up whole pubs and clubs – tramps came up to them in the street and danced for her. She *dazzled*. Other men always noticed her too, though they never seemed to notice him. She never made it clear enough that they were an item, he raged.

When she went back to her country, he vowed to follow her. He borrowed money, flew out, found a job that he hated teaching English (yet another stick he could beat her with). She had secretly hoped he wouldn't come, but resolved to try and make a go of it when he did. But he didn't get that her family needed her and she couldn't just move in with him. He said he wasn't ready to meet them anyway, but secretly fumed that she never invited him round.

But still: such memories! Such nights! Such passion! The sort of thing that happens only once in a lifetime. So, at least, he told everyone.

Then *such pain* when he called her from London, and she was in tears, and she said she'd not been well, and she really hadn't, but he didn't believe her. And then she ended up saying she'd met someone, because that was what he wanted to hear. And he hung up and never phoned her back.

And he couldn't *believe* that she'd done this to him.

And she couldn't believe that he didn't have it in him just to *wish her well*.

Ever after, down the years, his torch burned for her. He dreamt of her often, made impossible comparisons with other potential partners. (*Why would I want to compete with a myth?* said one, who didn't stick around.) She was his great impossible love, his grand obsession, his magnificent anecdotal agony. In his mind, he bore the pain of her absence with a quiet stoical pride. When, years later, he discovered via

141

Facebook that she was married with kids, he made friends take him out and console him. They did their duty by him, but he could tell they didn't get it.

But now, incredibly, more than three decades later, the great love of his life walked the same concourse as him once more. Manifest destiny! What a story – he could tell this one forever. And who knew where it might lead?

She approached from the main entrance, heading straight towards the ticket machines, from where she would double back to platform 11 and her train for the airport. He, meanwhile, had entered from the coach station side, putting him on a course at right angles to hers. Their paths would meet at a point about ten metres from the doughnut stand, where she – stopping to retrieve her ticket from her bag, and wondering aloud why she'd bothered to put it there when she knew she'd have to show it again almost straight away – would turn aside to make way as some man in a crumpled brown suit she'd once known, himself head down and staring vacantly ahead, made to move past her on the left.

She hadn't thought about him much at all in the intervening years. She had been far happier since, and sadder. She had raised a family, divorced, married again, got it right this time. She wasn't even sure she'd recognise him again, to be honest. He was just one of the mistakes that make up a life, and not even a favourite one.

He had married too, twice, and divorced, twice. He still blamed her for destroying his chances with anyone else. He had felt *so much* for her, he told people, that he had nothing left to give. She had made a dried-up husk of his heart. She had ruined his whole life, basically.

And so it was that, when the paths of the Great Lovers crossed that day in Victoria station, each was wrapped up in their own thoughts, neither noticed the other – and neither would ever know how close they had come to meeting again.

Not here, whispered the ticket machines. *Not now*, said the doughnut stand. *Not ever*, said the women in the purple sashes giving away free sample packs of a new brand of muesli bar.

ELLA G
IN A COUNTRY CHURCHYARD

The path from the cottage leads steeply up through a high tunnel formed by overhanging ash trees, and round to the cemetery they can see from the living-room window.

He can't quite remember how, but he and Ella have taken to walking up here every night of their week's holiday, in that restless, still-light half-hour before dinner that's otherwise filled with telly or handstands on the sofa or squabbles over access to the parental iPad. Mum made dinner and he cleaned up after; that was the usual holiday rule.

One trip to this flinty little Norman church had been enough for his other two children, but something about the gloomy mystique of the tombs and the musty drama of the dark Anglican interior has caught his seven-year-old daughter's magical imagination.

She – Ella, his Ella G – is wearing purple cords, a blue top with polka dots, and a red body-warmer. On her feet are her comfy white trainers with the Velcro fasteners; in her hand she absently carries a plastic green bottle of bubbles. She has dressed for the excursion; this is her churchgoing outfit.

*

They begin, as always, with a tour of the graves. She loves the big block capitals, the solemnly portentous messages carved out of solid granite. *In loving memory . . .; God be with you till we meet again . . .; Much-loved husband, dad, grandpa, friend, brother, uncle and teacher; 'To live in the hearts of those you love is not to die . . .'.*

'So this one's not dead, Daddy?'

'What's that, sweetie?'

'It says "not to die". So they put him in there even though he was still alive?' Her eyes flash with a sort of scandalised delight. These eyes that are the most alive thing he knows.

'Well, he is dead in one way,' he attempts. 'It's just that lots of people really loved him so he sort of still lives on in their hearts?'

'Ah!' she exclaims, her mind ablaze with instant under-standing. 'So he split in two, left the dead bit here and moved the living bit to the heart. Well, all the different hearts. So he had to split the living bit up again and again.'

'Yes, I guess so.' He prefers her explanation to his.

'And what does *reunited* mean?' She is pointing to a grave of two sisters, Rosalie and Florence, whom the stone says were 'reunited' on the latter's death, aged ninety-one years and three months.

'Well the first sister was on her own till the other died too,' he says. 'Now they can be together.'

'Sure. *Dead* together!' She snorts, though not unkindly.

'Well again, in each other's hearts . . .'

'Ah!' The eyes flash. 'So the bodies die but the hearts carry on living and they're in all the graves too.' It was not a question.

A woman shuffles past them with surprising speed. She is the only other person they have come across in all their trips. She has a fag on, which seems oddly blasphemous to him. Her face is blurry with tears.

'Why is she crying, Daddy?' Ella G stage-whispers.

'She's very sad because she's missing someone who's just died,' he replies.

'Doesn't she know about the hearts?'

'I think she does, it just takes a bit of getting used to not seeing the person around like before.'

Ella walks with exaggerated care around more graves. She finds the children's section. Here there are windmills to whizz and teddy bears to coo over.

'Look, Ella, this poor little girl died when she was just three months old.' Why on earth does he want to draw her attention to this? But he knows: it's the same impulse that prevents him from driving past a digger or a car transporter without pointing it out to his son.

'Daddy Daddy!' she cries in triumph, not to be outdone. 'Look!' He looks at the tiny grave and the awful words: *Our angel, who died aged just 15 minutes. 'And he will hold you in the palm of His hand.'*

'Who will hold you?' asks Ella, who must not die.

'God, I guess.' He is embarrassed by his lack of commitment to the answer.

'Oh. And who's he holding?'

'The little baby, I think.'

'Does he hold all the little babies who die?'

'I think he must do.'

She considers for a few moments. 'But that's OK,' she nods at last. 'Because God's got big hands.'

Another message jumps out at her. *Though you are so far away, we think of you 'most every day.* 'Daddy, Daddy! This one is the same as that other one!'

She's right. It's the third stone they've read with that wording. Perhaps like him, Ella had assumed that the messages on tombstones always dignified the dead with their originality. But now he sees that they are formulas, like greeting-card mottoes.

'When are you going to die, Daddy?' asks Ella tenderly.

He giggles awkwardly. He has had his brushes with mortality, but he sees now that he has learnt nothing that he can package as wisdom for his daughter. He remembers grief only as a dark cloud that the mind can never quite encompass, a wall that rises higher as you try in vain to vault it, an A3 concept that will not fold itself up into his paltry A4 envelope of a brain.

'Shall we go inside?' he says.

Inside all is dark and quiet and holy, stained-glass gloom. Three large rows of black organ pipes glower over one corner; unlit lamps hang on long cords from the high ceilings. Ella takes care not to walk on the worn tombstones embedded in the ancient tiled floor.

The church smells of furniture polish and cut flowers and a sort of dank earnestness. Sniffing the atmosphere, a phrase bubbles up at him from a student film review he once wrote: 'irretrievably Bergmanesque'.

The visitor's book, which they flicked through on their first visit, contains the usual selection of handwritten comments praising the 'beautiful country setting' and 'lovely prayerful atmosphere'. Only one message stands out, and Ella is always delighted to find it again. It says simply: '<u>Horrible</u> vicar'.

'Why is he horrible??'

'Maybe he wouldn't let people grow plants and flowers on the graves?'

'Or . . .' she says, brushing away his idea. 'Or *he was trying to steal the teddy bears.*'

Ella whizzes round the interior, which she has made completely her own. She looks at her reflection in the polished brass plaques honouring dead admirals and aldermen. Obsessively, she neatens the piles of hymnals and prayer-books at the end of every pew. She takes down each of the hassocks from its little hook – 'boosters', she calls them – and kneels on each in turn.

And, as always, she has them both climb the spiral steps to the top of the surprisingly elevated pulpit, where the same photocopied lyric sits waiting on the lectern. She is entranced by the words of this song, which she makes him photograph with his phone and sing the whole way through every time.

It seems vaguely sacrilegious to be standing in a pulpit singing *He's got the plants and the creatures in his hands* over and over into the dim, intense stillness of the empty church. But he is more superstitious about undermining this moment of communion with his daughter, so he sings with a sort of muted gusto.

Ella, who has quickly learnt the tune, is less inhibited. Her joyous chants ring out across the nave with indecent verve.

In a side chapel, on the way out, Ella spots a picture of Christ, thorns graphically embedded in his temples, his cheeks spotted with artfully positioned crimson drops. Underneath the Victorian image are these words in a strident Gothic typeface: *Glory to God in the Blood of the Cross.*

'Let's pray, Daddy!' He joins her at the kneeler. She stares wide-eyed at this impossibly glamorous image, this glimpse of forbidden knowledge.

'What is the Blood of the Cross, Daddy?'

'Well, Christians believed that Christ died to save them.'

'But what is the Blood of the Cross?'

'He bled when he died?' he says limply.

'Did the vicar kill him?'

'No. This was all a long time ago. Some nasty men hung him on a wooden cross and he died.'

'Is Christ's grave outside with the others, Daddy?'

'No,' he says, relieved that her butterfly mind has un-wittingly skipped the gory bit. 'Actually, he came back from the dead, and started to live again.'

'You mean, like *Astro Boy*?'

They had watched the film the night before, a manga-inflected tale of a father who brings his son back from the dead in the form of a robotic replica.

'*Exactly.*'

When they emerge back into the graveyard, the sky is darkening. The woman is still there, looking down at the same grave, fag-end glowing, still crying silently.

'Can ghosts go down into their graves and see their own bodies like on *Doctor Who*?'

He looks at his daughter, who is now making a bracelet with flowers from a battered graveside bouquet. He has brought her into a world in which she must die. He wishes with all his heart that it were not so, or that he could explain, or at least apologise.

He says: 'Ready for some sausages?'

PRODUCT RECALL NOTIFICATION

Category: Health & wellbeing

Product name: *Best Years of My Life™*

Brand: Penny's Own

Model number: DOB06121956

Recall date: Immediate

Description: Penny's Own brand wishes to recall its *Best Years of My Life™* product, which since its market launch in 1956 has been widely supplied by owner Penny Jennings to a range of partners, children and jobs. It is clearly defective because all these parties have squandered the love and care that were integral to the product's functionality for their own selfish ends. The product owner has been left wondering what the point of everything is, and wishes to recall her time so she can start again with a nicer set of people.

Detail: Well, hubby #1 fucked off at the first sign of a nappy, leaving her to raise the twins single-handed, while subsequent partner Bob (who didn't hold with marriage, on the grounds that 'we don't need a special day to tell each other how we feel') kept her and the kids dangling for twelve years with his on-off appearances before announcing, 'I just need to go and sit with myself for a while.' (According to recent Facebook posts, he is now married to a dentist in Canada who has five children from a previous marriage. Careful what you wish for, Bob!)

Hubby #2, Jean-Luc, was briefly promising, and things might have progressed there were it not for Penny's stubborn insistence that Jean-Luc should really have divorced wife #1 before their own whirlwind ceremony and honeymoon in Barbados. *Call me old-fashioned*, as she'd said when she found out, *but I've just always been a bit funny about bigamy*. She never did get all the credit-card money back.

On the work front, *Best Years of My Life*™ was supplied exclusively for twenty-seven years to the same garden centre business, where despite demonstrating extensive passion and knowledge, being adored by the customers, and single-handedly opening up a successful home delivery and e-commerce arm, Penny was repeatedly passed over for promotion in favour of Gareth, a dim, smelly lubbock whose only advantage over Penny was that he happened to be the boss's son.

As for Penny's twin children, Tom gets in touch about twice a year (usually when he needs some cash); Stacey on the other hand visits all the time, having blackmailed Penny into signing up as unpaid nanny for her grand-daughter Katya (the one good and pure thing to have come out of all this).

Other potentially affected products: Penny's Own Self-Esteem™, Penny's Own Bank Balance™, Penny's Own Energy Levels™, Penny's Own Faith in Humanity™ etc.

Risk: If you have been an ungrateful Best Years of My Life™ customer at some point, there is a small risk of having to face some difficult questions from the product owner. Things like: 'Did it ever occur to you to think about anyone but yourself?'; 'Do I have the word "mug" written across my forehead?'; or 'Where's my money, you thieving cut-price Lothario?'

Next steps: In the absence of a time machine or a karmic rebate on pearls squandered before swine, customers are advised that the best thing they can do now is probably to just leave Penny well alone. Or if you can't do that, maybe just try and be a bit more considerate in future? And if that's too much to ask, Penny's always been partial to a spot of Fruit & Nut.

CRUMBS

The cake sat in pride of place in the fridge, an ornate confection of glitter balls and sculpted chocolate frosting and sugar stars and gingerbread men done up as edible silver astronauts. It wasn't exactly *Bake Off* standard, but it had a certain enthusiastic seven-year-old's flair, and it was better than anything he could ever have done himself, as a child or an adult.

Mum had helped Lilly with the decorating and the baking, channelling her daughter's wild imaginings towards a realisable vision. The theme of the competition was Outer Space. The prize was an icing kit, and Lilly wanted it badly. He had suggested a recreation of the lunar landing, perhaps with a nod to the popular conspiracy theory that it had never really happened. To his surprise they had gone with that as a broad theme, although the module had proved too fiddly, and the fake-landing idea had proved a bit too close to home for a medium which – like embroidery or Ceefax imagery – could only ever aspire to a very approximate realism.

The kitchen was a happy mess when it was done. Lilly's face was smeared with icing sugar and chocolate, and there were pools of egg white and dusty patches of flour everywhere – emblems of a happy time, of hanging out with mum and a job well done.

The cake was moved with great ceremony onto a specially-emptied fridge shelf to set. Mum put out the fancy cake-tin it was to be placed in next morning. He had only one job: to get the cake to the table in the hall before the start of school, where it could be judged along with all the other entries.

All good! he said that night, from his seat at the PC. *Leave it to me.* He went in to the office late on Tuesdays, after doing the school drop. But first he'd have to work late tonight, to finish off the pitch deck. It was almost there, but he'd had some inputs in late from Tim and Chloe. Both were useful additions, but none of it as yet cohered; no one had gone to the trouble of making all the strands of their submission hang together as a logical fully-integrated argument, building to a powerful inescapable conclusion: *Hire us!*

The night was not easy. Jake, the youngest, was up three times complaining of pains in his ears, and that woke his sister. Lilly crawled into the bed with them some time in the wee blurry hours, and repeatedly broke into their slumber with her sleep-talking and her sleep-flailing. Mum had to get up on Tuesdays at 5.30am, and her alarm shocked him into consciousness at the very moment, or so it seemed, that he had finally reached the deep sleep he had been straining for the whole night.

'When I get up, I make a point of being with my children. I get them ready for school, and I am *present*. Work can wait.' So said, in a recent interview, the CEO of an early-stage fast-track tech company that was now entering hyper-growth and had been marked out by analysts as a potential unicorn. Said the CEO: 'If I check my email before I talk to my children in the morning, they *know*.' This was the same company his presentation pitch was designed to win over.

It was a wonderful idea, and one worth trying. One day. But he had been up till nearly 2am getting the deck to a place he could be happy with. Although at that point his eyeballs were melting and he'd have been grateful to still recognise wood as wood, never mind worrying about mixing it up with the trees, he had gone to bed with a quiet sense of great achievement. His own personal work-cake was in the oven, and he had a sneaking suspicion that he might just be Star Baker this week. If there was any early feedback, he wanted to know about it.

He stumbled into the kitchen and began the rituals of breakfast and pre-school prep. Every so often, he shouted out groggy bulletins urging his children to wake up, come downstairs, eat their food. Mum had stuck up helpful notes with messages such as 'Don't forget Lilly's swimming goggles' and 'Ask Miss Hankey if Jake can go up to next reading level'. The notes embarrassed him because (a) they made him feel like a hopeless bloke who couldn't organise basic family stuff himself, and (b) he was utterly dependent on them for getting through the next hour and a half.

Many of the movements were so familiar he could do them, as now, in his half-sleep. Beans in microwave. Bagels in toaster. Cut up apples. Shoes in pairs by door. Empty dishwasher, fill again. Drinks – hot milk for one, cold for the other. Porridge oats, Weetabix, a slice of chicken.

Then it was the scramble to get their clothes on and get them out the door in time. He had a system that he used, called the Big Five: Hair, Teeth, Bag, Shoes, Coat. 'Which of your Big Five haven't you done yet?' Actually it should really have been the Big Six, because Getting Dressed needed to be in there too, and that was often the hardest one of all.

Getting them up the stairs. Getting them to concentrate on their clothes, instead of drifting off to re-build their railway track (him) or re-arrange their squishies (her). It wasn't that they hadn't anything specific they'd rather be doing, though they were always up for anything with a screen. It was just that anything else was more interesting to them at that point than the one thing he actually needed them to be doing. Inevitably, there would be tears and screams and shouting. The kids didn't always behave very well either.

In the midst of all this, his phone vibrated in his dressing-gown pocket. It was a purple fluffy gown of his wife's which he always wore; he only allowed himself to get dressed after the kids were all done and stuck in front of the telly. He shouldn't look; there would be plenty of time for all that later. Remember what that CEO said. And she was a *CEO*.

He looked. It was from Dom, his own personal Paul Hollywood. He could tell from the subject line already – 'Urgent: Major concerns re deck' – that he was not in line for any special handshake this week. He sat on the edge of the bed, oblivious now to the escalating squabbles coming from the kids' bedroom next door.

Dom was indeed concerned about the deck. The whole thing was poorly paced. Visually, it was cliched. It was way too long. It said nothing that couldn't really have been said – and probably said much better – by any of our rivals. It was repetitive. There were gaps in the logic. And where it wasn't illogical, it was *banal*. As a result, Dom needed everyone to drop everything else they were doing and get in for a 10am stand-up when roles and tasks would be assigned to fix this mess.

There were howls of pain and anger from next door now, but he didn't hear them.

He went down to his PC, opened up his email, and began drafting a furious reply. He was very surprised by Dom's response, he began with deceptive mildness. He had put a huge amount of work into the deck, at great personal cost, and he stood by what he had done. He believed the client would be impressed by the dexterity of the argumentation and would gratefully discern, as Dom had clearly failed to, the subtle nuances of its movements, and how each strand both answered a specific point of the brief and also demonstrated by implication how each of their key competitors would not be as well placed to deliver on its requirements. Did Dom even get what the client wanted? Was he even looking at the right version of the deck? Was Dom determined, in short, to carry on being a fucking annoying moronic twat?

A scream from upstairs, too loud even for him to ignore. He clicked off his PC. This was an email he would never send. And besides, it was 8.47.

8.47! *Fuck*. He raced upstairs, roughly disentangled his fighting children, and began combing hair and scraping teeth and pulling on trousers with the energy of only-just-suppressed violence. He dragged the children into the car, and they had torn halfway down the hill before Lilly pointed out that they had left the cake behind.

Swearing quietly but intensely, he executed a neat *Sweeney*-esque turn and pointed the car back round the block to their house. He double-parked, sprinted in, shoved the cake in its tin, picked up his vital laptop and work-bag – which he discovered now he'd also forgotten – and drove off fast, much faster than the roads round his home allowed.

At the bottom of the hill, the turn to the right was one you could lean into without slowing when cycling; he tried the same in his car now, but was forced to brake very sharply when an Ocado van emerged unseen from the left. The children lurched forward, folding horribly forward for a split-second over their belts. And the plastic bag with the cake-tin in flew off the front seat and rolled over and over in the footwell.

Outside the school, he kangarooed the car awkwardly past smug post-drop-off parents and in and out of side roads, looking for an elusive space. But everywhere – even the semi-dodgy spots, on private areas and resident-only slipways – was taken. In the end there was nothing for it but to park the Kangoo in the very nearest road, in front of the driveway of a man who had shouted at him only last week for parking in front of his driveway.

Next came the Sweaty Breathless Jog of Shame, up the pathway into school in the face of more smug parents who'd got it together enough this morning – and no doubt every morning, the smug staring fuckers – to get their kids to class on time. Once Jake had been dropped at his class, after some desperate knocking on the glass door – and after he had even remembered to ask about Jake's reading level, though he had no recall now of what Miss Hankey's response had been – he and Lilly whizzed frantically round to the school hall.

The lollipop lady – an enduring and much-loved figure, who enjoyed minor celebrity status in the local community – had agreed to judge the cakes. Cake deadline: 9am. Time now: 9.12am. But there had to be a grace period. There was always a fucking grace period. Sure enough, the lady from the office smiled at Lilly, and made a space for her offering. Her dad opened the tin and inspected the contents.

It was total devastation inside. One astronaut had been beheaded; the other had been broken into three pieces, all embedded now at awkward angles in brown sugary mud. The carefully sculpted chocolate lunarscape had attached itself smearily to the inside of the tin lid. The decorative stars and balls and planets had all fallen off or stuck to the sides where they didn't belong, so that none of the constellations that mum and Lilly had spent so long recreating could be made out. The artful surface crater no longer worked either, not now that the cake was essentially all crater.

Or rather cakes. He pulled out the four main pieces it had broken into, and tried to arrange them into some semblance of a pattern. Then he added the smaller pieces around them in a rough orbit of cake asteroids. Then, for want of anything else to do, he poured the thick layer of crumbs from the bottom of the tin over the remnants of his daughter's Outer Space-themed competition entry.

Next to her ex-cake, the other entries bore extraordinary witness to hour upon hour of tender kitchen artistry. There was a space galaxy cake, atop which meringue planets – all shaped to scale, all decorated according to current astronomical knowledge of each celestial body's respective surface – revolved around a marzipan sun. There was an intricate space shuttle in mid-launch, whose great billows of smoke turned out to be wonderfully plumed cupcakes. Someone had created an ingenious space beach with the help of popcorn, Cheerios and crushed honeycomb. There was a giant rocket made with five different colours of sponge, and another marbled wonder that recreated that famous shot of the world as seen from space.

In short, there was evidence everywhere of mums and dads who cared enough about their kids to get their cakes to school unbroken. He felt a sudden stab of hatred at Dom, and another at the infuriatingly chirpy lollipop lady.

He wondered what was worst. The pitying look on the face of the lady from the school office? The forthcoming row with the driveway man? The realisation that he was still wearing his pyjama trousers? But really, there was no competition. His daughter's face – on which the dark night of extreme disappointment was already turning dawn-like into an expression of almost cosmic forgiveness – easily won that prize.

THE ANGRY SUN GOD

'Where's the Big Purple Dinosaur Bus, Daddy?'

'I had to take it in to get it fixed, sweetie. Do you want some Hula Hoops?'

It was Tuesday of half term, my day off from the super-market, and we were on the bus to Thornhurst. They had a decent soft play and a pool with slides there, and it was one of Alfie's favourite places. We often came here on weekends in the van – I suppose it's the divorced dad's equivalent of the zoo in my part of the world. Followed by McDonalds, obviously.

I hadn't been on a bus for a long time, but I realised that this could be the first trip of many. Not only did I have no licence, I still had no van. And even if I got it back, I doubt if I'd ever be able to drive it again.

Climbing to the top deck took me right back – back to my old days of taking this very bus route to school with my mates. Sitting up front by the funny periscope thing you could look down and see the top of the driver's head in. The trees crashing against the roof and scratching down the sides as we made our way through the forest roads. The hard nuts setting fire to stuff down the back. The time I opened my surprisingly heavy bag to find Jacko had put a large and still very live crab in it.

That morning Janine first kissed me in front of everyone, her way of telling the world (and me) that we were an item. My childhood sweetheart – now my ex-wife.

In the soft play, Alfie runs straight in, flicking off his shoes as he goes, and heads off up the nearest tower of webbing and foam. Normally this'd be a prime chance for me to grab a cappuccino and start dicking about on my phone. But I'm not looking for alone time right now, so I throw off my trainers too and follow him in.

Inside, I dodge the swinging punch bags, jump across the vinyl stepping stones, and bend down to move through a dark section decked out with Halloween imagery. My aim is to catch up with Alfie at the enclosed rope bridge across the middle, so we can climb up the rope steps and jump down the mini death slide together. A song sticks in my head:

> *Faraway girl, crying in the rain*
> *Faraway girl, alone with her pain*

I'd forgotten about the rollers. To get into the higher, central area of the soft play, you have to sideways-slide your whole body through these two giant rollers. Easy for a kid, but if you're an uninitiated adult you feel as though you're going to bust your ribs and crush all your inner organs if you carry on with the roll. Or, worse, you can just get stuck there, especially if there's a sharp turn just after the rollers, which is what happened to Janine's mum once. We all just stood laughing our heads off while she had a panic attack.

In doing these manoeuvres you can't help coming up close and personal with lots of other people's random kids. Most of them ignore you, but sometimes you get an arsey one who wants to know what you're doing in their territory. Here's one now.

'This is a war zone!!!' he screams. 'GET OUT NOW!'

There's nothing playful in his expression. He's like a bailiff or a bouncer, with the nasty, smug look of a bully whose natural aggression is licensed by his job. 'GET OUT OF THE WAY!'

He's a little Malfoy, with blond hair and a sort of permanent snarl to his upper lip. I know enough about kids' clothes to know that his are casually, trendily expensive too.

But I'm stuck. I've gone in the rollers at an angle, and now my ankle won't twist round enough to get me free.

'GET OUT!' he screams again, his face screwed up with rage. Posh thugs are the worst.

'You're very rude,' I begin, but my voice is trembling and my eyes are welling up.

Sensing weakness, he closes in and starts to pelt my head and face with hollow plastic balls from the ballpit. I cradle my head in my arms and lie there as the balls rain down on me. Other boys join in.

I lie there and think of nothing. I want them to keep throwing.

Then I hear a tiny scared voice: '*Leave my daddy ALONE!*'

It is Alfie's voice, fearful and high-pitched, a few feet off.

I sit up to see my five-year-old son's face peering at me through plastic mesh. His dad is being pelted by a gang of nasty eight-year-olds, and he is terrified, both for me and for him. But he will not leave me.

My son's face is awful to look at. I can see he is shaking. His face is stained with tears (like mine), and I know how hard his heart will be beating. He daren't approach the bigger boys but he can't bear to leave his dad on the battlefield either.

I fight my way free of the roller, bat away the balls – which really sting now, being thrown at point blank range by the little fuckers, and surprisingly hard – and escape the war zone to the edge of the rope walkway, where Alfie crouches amid the ruins of his weekend.

I hold him and hug him and tell him sorry over and over.

I cannot forgive myself. No one can be brave unless he feels fear, as Alfie and I both know from *The Lion King*. But thanks to his so-called dad, he has had to find this out the hard way.

I have a silly thing about water, I sort of believe that it *cleanses* as well as cleans, that it heals the spirit as well as eases the body. I suppose it goes back to all those baptisms I served at as a boy, all those babies screaming as the scallop shell of water splashes onto their forehead. Plus all the jugs of water I saw poured into chalices, all those readings about bathing in the River Jordan, water that turns into wine etc.

And when he came up out of the water, immediately he saw the heavens opening and the Spirit descending on him like a dove. All that.

After Dad died I went swimming all the time – even got mum to come with me sometimes – and it really helped us get through those early days. So, after the soft play fuck-up – and with all that has happened – I'd been looking forward to taking to the waters of Thornhurst with Alfie.

But the kids' pool was so rammed we ended up getting into the shallow end of the big pool, something neither of us was keen to do as it felt like it was about twenty degrees colder. Alfie had on his Paw Patrol armbands plus the extra support of a fluorescent green foam noodle tied loosely round his middle.

He'll be a good swimmer; his lessons are really starting to pay off. He's got a strong kick and he's just starting to suss that he can control the direction he travels in the water. We chugged up and down, me pulling him by the arms, encouraging him to motor along under his own steam, making paddles of his hands to scoop through the water. He did a few jumps from the side, aiming his taut little body straight at my head. Then I got him to try a few strokes on his back.

Then a man leant over from poolside and pushed me in the face.

I lost my footing, lost hold of Alfie, slipped under water. For a split second I looked up and saw all the legs above me pumping away, all those little bodies afloat on that precarious tide.

All the feet kicking for dear life.

I got back above the surface, ready to scour the pool in a panic for Alfie. But he was right there, bobbing about, the terrified look on his face again. I turned to the man, braced for more.

But he'd lost all interest in me. He was leaning over to guide a little boy, doubtless his own son, to safety. The boy was spluttering water, panicked and nearly submerged, but in the press of bodies no one had noticed this small potential tragedy unfold, and we'd strayed between the man and the boy he was trying to save. I watched immobile as at last he yanked him out to safety.

Now with the boy safe, the man turned to me again.

'Let him drown, would yer, you fuck?' he said, as he led the boy off to his waiting, tearful mother.

'I didn't know . . .' I tried to say. 'He just . . .'

But he never gave me another look. I watched his ripped torso and the giant tattoo of an astrological sun that stretched taut across his whole long back.

In his sculpted perfection, his anger, his disdain, his heroism, he was like a god. A god that I had displeased. I could feel other eyes now, boring into me from around the pool. And in that one moment the whole point and pleasure of our trip to the pool's healing waters was squashed dead.

A sun tattoo. A flash of scarlet. A click. A sausage dog. A cordon of police tape. A pile of bouquets in cellophane.

I just wanted to get us out of the pool now, but I didn't want to meet Sun Man again. So we puttered about in the water a bit more, not even half-heartedly, spent a long time in the shower, and even longer changing in our cubicle.

Alfie wanted another packet of Hula Hoops from the vending machine on the way out. They cost 75p, but I didn't have the change. As we were dithering by the machine, a girl in a tracksuit put in 75p. Alfie instantly pressed the code for the Hula Hoops.

'That wasn't for you!' I snapped. 'Jesus Christ! Not everything in the whole world is run for your benefit! Say sorry!!' I was almost hysterical. The only thing I'm pleased about here – and this is a paltry plus – was that I managed not to say 'whole *fucking* world'. I *think*.

'It's OK. He can have them,' said the girl, who was clearly less worried about her 75p and more scared of what I'd do to my child next. Alfie was trembling silently now, fighting back tears for all he was worth.

I apologised for what had happened over and over, insisted she wait while I went to the reception, changed a tenner and got her her money back. But it was pretty obvious to both of us that it wasn't Alfie I was apologising for.

All of this had taken my mind off the Sun Man. But now the veil of dread came down again, and I slinked over to the bus stop followed at a short distance by my son, who hadn't spoken since and was now sat on the shelter's red plastic bench with a Hula Hoop on the end of each of his fingers.

'Daddy,' he said, sucking thoughtfully on one of his original-flavour rings of shaped potato crisp.

'Yes, my man?'

'What happened to that little girl?'

'Which little girl?' I squeezed my nose to try and get rid of the ache in my ears.

'The one you knocked down with your van.'

My eyes sting and my ears still ache. A car drives past, slow enough for me to see Sun Man in the passenger seat, staring straight ahead.

THE APPEAL

'How, then, would you describe your wife?'

'Oh she's OK. If you like that sort of thing.'

'Is that all?' said the Global Confederation Inspector, a brisk, alarmingly tall woman who sat between two silent and much shorter male assistants before a neat row of flat screens. 'She has performed exceptionally well in all our eligibility tests and screening exercises. She's in the highest percentile for EQ, IQ, verbal reasoning, logic, cognition, physical fitness, applied mechanics . . .'

'Applied mechanics?' he snorted. 'She doesn't even know where the screenwash goes.'

'She'll make a very effective mission team member, by all available predictive and psychometric indices.'

'In some lights,' he said warningly, 'she looks like Lennie the Lion. It's the hair.'

He had written to the Appeals Commission in confidence, saying that he had strong grounds for his wife to be de-selected from the mission to Mars. But he could tell from the Inspector's blank expression that his arguments had yet to strike home.

'She has oddly intimate relationships with cacti,' he continued. 'Some of them have lasted longer than our marriage.'

His wife didn't know he'd written. She'd told him she didn't really want to go, but she had such a strong sense of duty that she'd never back out of a commitment. She was an optimist too – she believed all their guff about a Bold Step Forward for all.

The Inspector touched a screen. 'Yeees. We were impressed by her evident horticultural faculties. On top of her myriad other competencies, of course.'

'She talks to courgette plants! She makes important life decisions by consulting a weather app!'

He suspected that she was secretly excited by the idea of being a Planetary Pioneer. What he couldn't stomach was the thought that she might secretly want some time away from him.

'That sort of meteorological vigilance will be a vital life skill on Mars,' said the Inspector crisply. 'Though we have stabilised the atmosphere within the bio-colony, the artificial microclimate remains at odds with the prevailing weather system, and conditions may not always be hospitable.'

'She needs a man to carve the chicken! She's addicted to gory films she can't actually watch! She can't look at a bed without insisting on changing the sheets!'

'Are you going to tell us about the murky depths of her handbag next?'

'Yes! No one knows what vile creatures lurk in there!' He stopped, startled. 'But how could you possibly know that?'

'Oh, you'd be surprised how often the husbands mention the handbag at this point,' said the Inspector, a touch complacently. 'But really, I don't understand your attitude. Your wife has been selected to help humanity settle on a new planet – and she's accepted of her own free will. Working with all our other brave Planetary Pioneers, she will help enable our race to start a new life on a new world. You should be very proud!'

'Earrings make her look like a man,' he snarked.

'I really can't see the issue,' sighed the Inspector. 'You don't even have children. Which is, of course, another great plus.'

He looked at the floor.

'And it's not as if we're taking her away *for ever*, is it?'

Wasn't it? Ever since they'd started the first pilot colonies on Mars, the time it took to get there had been rapidly coming down, from years to months and now weeks, they said. But why didn't anyone ever seem to come back?

'If you wake her up in the night,' he said, with fresh inspiration, 'she can be *quite violent*.'

'Oh *do come on*,' said the Global Confederation Inspector, throwing her pen down.

His mind was racing. Even if he did manage to sum up what she really meant to him, as he had failed to do in every birthday or anniversary card he'd ever tried to write her, wouldn't that just make them want her all the more?

'She cycles in and out of parked cars! She likes country and western music!! *She'll only eat curry with a spoon!!!*'

No response.

'She gets super-stressed whenever she has to do a presentation at work,' he bitched. 'She always claims she'll never pull through.'

The Global Confederation Inspector leaned forward for once. 'And then what happens?'

He sighed helplessly. 'Oh she produces yet another remarkably cogent piece of work, several days in advance, and blows everyone away with her quietly fierce intelligence.'

'I see.'

He felt suddenly exhausted, like everyone kept saying his planet was. All of humanity would probably need to migrate to Mars eventually, the Global Confederation said. Too much bad stuff had happened on the Earth, too many resources wasted, too much geopolitical baggage. This was a chance to start again, to wipe the slate, to make a Bold Leap Forward for all. And of course they wanted to send the best people first, the Planetary Pioneers, to get things ready for the rest.

Only – and this was the other question that bugged him – what was to stop them 'accidentally' pulling up the space drawbridge, leaving him and the rest of the deadbeats behind? Like in that Douglas Adams book?

'She'll say she doesn't want any chips,' he said with quiet malice. 'And then she'll steal yours.'

'Marvellous!' said the Global Confederation Inspector. 'Frugality *and* initiative.'

'She bites her toenails.'

'Resourceful!'

He was desperate now. 'She has the sort of compassionate soul that makes you want to be a better person! Her cryptic-crossword face has a sort of quizzical nobility that makes you want to take her in your arms and squeeze her forever!'

The Global Confederation Inspector also looked quizzical. 'I thought you were trying to convince me *not* to send her to Mars?'

'I am,' he sighed. 'But I can't think of a bad thing to say about her.'

'She certainly seems like a . . . a very special person,' said the Inspector. 'Which is why we selected her of course. As I say, she'll make a very effective team member. It's a great honour.'

'She is not *effective*,' he replied, in spite of himself. 'She is *everything*.'

'Excellent!' smiled the Global Confederation Inspector, blithely tapping a screen. 'We'll inform you of the outcome of your appeal in due course.'

His heart dropped. He knew what that meant.

'In the meantime, we'll progress your wife's induction programme to its conclusion just in case your appeal is, ah, unsuccessful,' said the Global Confederation Inspector. 'There are just a few formalities and final checks now. A final medical, some insurance paperwork. The firework test and so on.'

'The firework test?'

His mind took him back to their honeymoon: out with the crowds on Independence Day in Mexico City. It was in this gaudily dramatic land, where throwing bangers across unlit streets at unsuspecting gringos is a national pastime, that he had chanced upon his bride's innermost fear.

'Oh yes,' the Global Confederation Inspector was saying. 'Going where she's going, she'll need to be OK with a few loud bangs and flashes.'

'*I don't know how you can live with yourself!*' he hissed smugly.

THE VIRTUAL WRITER

Once, in about 2001, Mack and me were in the pub, discussing the issue of getting down to the writing once again. Mack had a plan.

His ageing auntie ran a pub in the country, and Mack suggested we take the place over. We'd get up early every day to sign off the deliveries, do a morning's work on our novs, then run the pub in the evening. Each of us would spur the other on, the fictional equivalent of gym buddies. What could go wrong?

Mack was very, very serious. We had both worshipped since forever at the altar of literature – Mack, indeed, was famous for claiming that TS Eliot understood him better than any person alive. And we had both been on the verge of penning something important since at least 1985, when we'd met in college.

When you get the call from me at your office tomorrow, be ready, said Mack. *I'll have called my aunt and jacked my job in. You'll need to resign too and we'll head off to Shropshire tomorrow.*

Are you up for this, Jon? Do you really want this, Jon? Because if we shake hands now, there's no going back.

We didn't get blood out or anything – we weren't the type – but we did a lot of mutual chest-stabbing of an intense pub kind.

Next day, I told my closest colleagues with an awkward smirk, might well be my last. I had made an oath, and I would have to follow through. But Mack, who had a six-figure salary at an international headhunting agency that kept him in coke and 'poo and glamorously self-destructive girlfriends, never called.

We don't meet up much nowadays. It's not really because our lifestyles are less compatible, though it's convenient to think so. It's because, after almost three decades, the talk of getting down to the writing is starting to ring a tad hollow.

Last time I saw Mack, he'd signed up for a series of expensive seminars with a top screenwriting guru. He said he enjoyed the talks, but couldn't get on with the assignments. One can only watch in awe, for the vocation of virtual writer is far, far harder than actual writing could ever be.

Let us be clear. Virtual writers are not people who don't write; rather, they are people who are about to write, who haven't written yet, who are writers in all but the writing. They are people who care so much about writing – about writing well – that they can't quite bring themselves to start. Their confidence eroded by over-exposure to the masters, their will sapped by the wet cuddle of booze, things are nevertheless always about to change.

It takes inhuman reserves of persistence and ingenuity to fall short of one's dream so hard and so often. Virtual writers like Mack are fucking heroes, and the books they have not written are fucking masterpieces, virtually.

THE BEACH SHOP

Even if I've been up late running the disco the night before, I always have to be in at seven to get the bread ovens up and running, let the bloke with the papers in, sign off any deliveries, and ready the all-essential coffee machine. *Nom de dieu*, this isn't exactly what you'd call a stressful job. Knackering, sure, but stressful, no. Except . . . imagine what it'd be like if there was no coffee or baguettes here one morning. The campers would riot.

By quarter to eight, the usual little crowd was forming. Men, almost all of them. *Britanniques* and *allemands*, mostly. While the rest of the campsite sleeps, the early birds form an approximate but single-minded queue outside my beach shop, waiting for their fix of coffee and a moment of space, a clandestine *pain au chocolat* and a day-old *Daily Mail*.

There's the jogger who always tries to time the end of his run with the opening of the shop at 8am. Tanned legs, fancy running shoes, slick headphones, receding hairline, metallic shades . . . he gives off the air of a man losing a desperate race against time. He always finishes his run too early, paces up and down on the sand till we pull the shutters up, then frets in the line-up for his *baguettes*, crashing the sleepy

173

morning vibe with his fidgety impatience and his twitchy smiles that aren't really smiles.

'You're supposed to be on holiday, aren't you?' I want to say to him. 'What are you running from?'

The old guy with the surgical stockings is another regular this week. He's both very tall and rather portly, which makes him look like a small, post-operative giant. Every morning he strides painfully past the shop and down to the beach with his support sticks, sliding gingerly across the sand like a minor ski deity bereft of snow. Like everyone in my morning crowd, his order is religiously consistent: *deux pains au chocolat et une rustiguette*, in his case. Then the painful limp back to his chalet, another small step towards recovery ticked off.

There's one woman among the regulars, a mum. She pushes a fancy buggy with a sleeping infant in a prone position. Her pale face – and especially her crumpled eyes – tell the story of a blurry succession of broken nights, of endless walking up and down to soothe a crying child. Wake this child up now, her exhausted but resolute expression says, and I won't be responsible for my actions. It's another fine morning by the sea, the weather is looking lovely again, as it has all week, the sky is a deep poignant blue, and the bread is still warm. But for this woman, you can see, the day's small agonies are only just beginning.

Next up is the unshaven, paunchy bloke who always orders five *baguettes* and two *croissants aux amandes*. Don't mention those to the wife, he always says, with a sly wink. I've never met your wife, I always want to say back. No doubt she's put him on some forbidding diet – albeit a very timely one, looking at his bulging stomach. Probably got a few kids back at the caravan, so they can make sandwiches for lunch before they head off for the day's cycle ride, and still have a *baguette* left to go with dinner.

He always insists on trying his French out, this one, and buys the local *Journal du Sud-Ouest* rather than the *Mail*. Seems ashamed to be recognised as English – he even tried apologising for Brexit on his second morning. Like anyone cares about that shit over here, I want to tell him. It's nothing to do with us – just sort yourselves out and stop moaning. And have a fucking shave, *monsieur*. His uneven beard – a badge of being on holiday, no doubt – looks scraggier by the day. It's got a weird white stripe in it which makes me think of a mangy badger.

At 7.30, Jeanette and Thierry join me. Thierry and I fucked the first week of the season, after the World Cup disco. It was a bit awkward after that, but it's OK now. Neither of us had wanted more, I don't think, but each was terrified that the other did. (First rule of holiday camp: never get jiggy with another staffer at the start of the season. Shag in haste – repent at leisure.) A couple of weeks of blanking each other had ironed things out, though, and we were back on normal speaking terms now. I see Thierry is sniffing round Magalie these days, bringing her drinks by the poolside when she's life-guarding and slavishly carrying all the mats down to the beach for her yoga sessions.

Poor Magalie, it's the same every summer. She's irresistible to all the blokes, staff and campers alike. You're lucky, you can have your pick, I said to her once. But I don't want to be irresistible, she said, I want to be *complètement inapprochable*, and I saw what she meant.

Magalie didn't have a problem with having flawless skin or a pretty face or a fine figure, she wasn't coy about her looks and she dressed to express herself. But she wasn't a flirt or a tease or any of those other made-up crimes that men hurl at women who don't want to sleep with them. She was just kind and upbeat and attractive, and she had a smile for everyone. As a result – and this is what did her head in – every single male in the camp seemed to think that he was in his rights to have a crack at her. It wasn't anything she did, it was just something they saw, or thought they saw, something achey and desperate they all projected onto her.

Every summer, Magalie had the same sort of crap. That sailing instructor who'd called her a *sale pute* and a *pouffiasse* for leading him on (She hadn't. And so what if she had?). A clumsy punch-up between two campers who both thought they were in with her. An uncomfortable moment on a staff night out at the end of last summer when the ageing *patron's* oldest son Yves, who it was rumoured would soon take over the place, tried to kiss her. She got an apology of sorts later, from M Dubois himself, but still.

What none of them knew – and I'd been sworn to secrecy about it – was that Magalie had been with the same guy for years. An older guy, who lived in Paris with a second home on the island. Married, albeit in name only. A politician of some sort. He couldn't get divorced for reasons that were also political, apparently. She only worked here so she could spend time with him. It sounded like a crap arrangement to me but she said it was what she wanted.

Once the early birds had been served, the ovens were on and the papers were out, there was always a bit of a lull. I sometimes did a quick tour of the shop, noting stock gaps, facing up shelves and generally trying to make our wares look a bit more appetising. Beyond the essentials like bottled water and red wine and insect repellent and suncream and buckets & spades, our *articles de plage* had a dusty, naff feel: dubious blue straw hats, grotesquely leering inflatable unicorns, ancient postcard views of implausibly tinted sky and sea. The coast was pretty in these parts, but nowhere looked like *that*. We had fluffy sand, true, and frothy diagonal waves that were great for boogie-boarding toddlers and junior surfers. But we also had rocks in awkward spots and too much seaweed and the odd unsightly high-rise on the other side of the bay and too much litter.

Actually I preferred the reality; there's something oppressive about perfection.

I popped out the front for a smoke. Other people's holidays bore me. The tide of people trying to have fun washed in and out all day, and I longed for something different to happen. A freak thunderstorm. A whale sighting. The discovery of a dead body on the beach.

Monsieur Brexit was still sitting, with his third *grand crème*, at one of the little rickety tables outside the shop. His hair fell into two lank wings, separated by a centre-parting a long way up his forehead. He'd twigged early in his stay that the shop coffee was cheaper than the prices at the bar over by the pool, so he hung around, milking his moment of freedom and furtively scoffing his pastries. His five *baguettes* sat next to him, the paper bags soggy with the overnight dew that had collected on the glass surface.

'Careful you don't get your bread wet,' I called. I said it in French; he was the sort of bloke who'd be hurt if you spoke to him in his English, it was a pride thing. It took him a while to process my words, though, and you could almost see the cogs whirring.

'*Absolument!*' he said hurriedly. '*Les gosses ne me le*' – a big pause – '*ne me le . . . pardonneraient jamais!*' The kids would never forgive me. Fair play to him, I thought. The conditional third person plural can't be easy for a *rosbif*. And it's nice to see someone making a bit of an effort.

I pictured his kids. Three crazy boys, I decided, running around and shouting and throwing stuff. Competing for everything, fighting non-stop, devouring everything in sight but still always hungry. My brothers, basically. They'd probably just be getting up as he was coming back, and they'd pounce on the bread and devour it in seconds.

'Leave some for me and your mum!' he'd call weakly, slumping in his plastic chair on the verandah of their cabin. (I was sure he wouldn't be camping; I just couldn't imagine him under canvas.)

'It doesn't matter,' she'd say quietly. 'At least they're not hitting each other.' His wife, I suddenly thought: perhaps she's French? *Mais non. Impossible.* A French woman would never let her man run to seed like that.

Over by the pool, the yummy mummies were readying themselves for Magalie's morning session of Aquarobics. Thierry was over there already, obsequiously moving chairs and testing the sound system. I saw Monsieur Brexit head off through the wet area, then make an abrupt about-turn and start walking back through the gate, down the beach path, the long way back to the accommodation areas. Perhaps his wife was doing the class, and he was supposed to have been back to supervise the kids ages ago? Or was he supposed to be doing the class himself, and just couldn't be arsed? Either way, I fancied he was heading for the dog-house.

'*Alors, hier, ça a été monsieur?*' How was yesterday?

'*Oh oui, oui, très bien!*' enthuses Monsieur Brexit. '*Quelle belle journée!*' He is chipper this morning, and I find myself imagining his wife has surprised him with some early-morning nookie. She's a night person as a rule, I tell myself, but is usually too knackered at the end of the day to think about sex. Whereas he's a morning person, though he rarely gets the chance. On holiday, however, she was prepared to make the odd exception, and she'd certainly put a smile on his face today.

They'd had a great time yesterday, he was telling me now. The kids had really got into the cycling, and even the youngest had kept going all day with his little wheels and lack of gears. They'd followed the coast path all the way round the headland as far as the lighthouse – *jusqu'a la Phare!!* – and had stopped off for oysters and a glass of Muscadet on the way home. Happy, tired children, music from a traditional little *orchestre*, a beautiful sunset and a gentle breeze . . . *C'était magnifique!*

His French is really quite good, I have to admit. But it's the genders that always betray them. *Phare* (lighthouse) is masculine, I'm afraid. Always will be.

Oysters. Classic aphrodisiac, they say. Then my imagination stopped short. I don't know why I keep feeling the urge to fill in these people's days in my head like this, I guess it's just boredom. But I found that my mind drew the line at imagining Monsieur Brexit in bed.

He's started ordering two or three coffees at once now, so he doesn't have to keep queueing up again. Today we also had an in-depth discussion on French coffee terminology. What precisely, he wanted to know, is the difference between a *café au lait* and a *crème* and a *double espresso avec lait chaud?* What indeed, I wanted to say. But instead, I said: '*Oh c'est compliqué, ça!*' which turned out to be just what he wanted to hear. French was a mystical pleasure to him, an elusive mistress who would lead him on but never fully yield to his comprehension, and I'd accidentally conjured up for him a whole universe of subtle gastronomic nuance that a mere Anglo-Saxon could never hope to penetrate. And that, of course, was exactly how he liked it.

Next morning, he looked more unkempt and knackered than ever. He wore a dull black T-shirt sporting a rock band's faded logo, a pair of green Bermuda shorts, and brown Velcro sandals that crassly highlighted his pinky-white, toneless British legs. He ordered only his coffees and his pastries this time.

'*Vous ne voulez pas de baguettes ce matin, monsieur?*' I asked. It was rare for my early birds to modify their regular order midweek, but common enough for them to be too hungover to remember it all.

'Oh yeah, sorry. Go on then,' he said, in muttered English.

Later, as he sat under the parasol at his rickety table, perspiring heavily and dodging the morning sun like a beached turtle, I saw him whip a small bottle of vodka from his pocket and add a good slug to his coffee. *Monsieur Brexit!* I thought. *Vous êtes trop rock 'n' roll!*

Subtly I pointed him out to Thierry. 'He's starting early today.'

'Oh that one, he's a fruitcake,' said Thierry.

'How do you mean?'

'He hired an *électrique royale* from me for the week.' (We all wear several hats on camp, and one of Thierry's is running the cycle hire.) 'It's the most expensive bike we've got – only worth forking out for if you're going long distances, like the whole *circuit de l'île*, you know? But all he does every day is about fifty laps of the campsite. Just goes round and round, up all the little pathways, like a madman. Like he's afraid to leave the site.'

'Is he on his own? No family with him?'

'Always on his own. He's freaking out all the parents in the playground. They've started to think he's spying on their kids or something.'

'Jesus. Where's he staying?'

'Over in the Blue area somewhere, I think.'

'What – he's in a tent?'

'Think so, yeah. Magalie says she saw him trying to dry his smalls on a disposable barbecue yesterday.'

I looked over at Monsieur Brexit. His face was mostly in shadow, his shoulders drooping, the fuzzily striped stubble scuzzier than ever. Perhaps I imagined it, but it looked for a moment as if he were quietly crying into his third *grand crème*.

It was Thursday when it happened, I think. A usual early-morning start for me, bread and deliveries and a wave to Serge the cut-price Surf School Lothario as he quad-biked past in a flash of bleached hair, ultrabrite teeth and fake tan.

As the early birds gathered outside the still-shuttered shop, and we busied ourselves with unloading loaf trays, counting out the float for the till and coating the espresso machine, we heard a commotion outside. Through the window we made out shouts and some scuffles. I ran to the door.

Two men were pushing each other around, feet scratching for purchase on the sand. One was panting heavily, head down and arms clasped around the waist of the other man as if he'd just charged him and got stuck there. I knew at once it was Monsieur Brexit. The other, taller and stronger, was trying to push him back with two hands applied to his assail-ant's forehead. Monsieur Brexit was rapidly losing ground; under the pressure from his opponent – who I saw now was Twitchy Jogging Man – his head and neck were being pushed further and further back, at an angle to his shoulders that was starting to look all wrong.

As with all fights, it took a moment for people to react. You could call it shock, as we all stood there and tried to process this awkward violation of normality; I think a more honest word might be enjoyment. There is always something fascinating about other people fighting, other people's pain.

Thierry and Serge had come over, and the pair were quickly separated. Jogging Man was angry but I could see he was mostly mystified. What had he ever done to this bloke? Monsieur Brexit, meanwhile, sat on a pile of kids' boogie boards, with his head in his hands, making a sort of im-possible noise that I can only describe as a quiet howl.

Slowly but surely, though, the unpleasantness subsided, and the sleepy holiday vibe took hold once more. But for once at least the staff of the *Boutique de la Plage* had something to discuss other than who was sleeping with who, or when was Dubois ever going to deliver on his promised pay rise, or which campers had had cosmetic work done, or the Thierry-Magalie situation. Sometimes that's all 'romance' seemed to be, after all: men clutching clumsily at women, and women finding ways to let them down without damaging their fragile egos.

It was the following morning that Monsieur Brexit's wife appeared. Or ex-Mme Brexit, as it turned out. She was a regular in the shop after lunch – I recognised her from the pretty jewelled hairband and high bun she always wore. She was striding down to the beach, two young girls in tow, when she looked across and saw him at his preferred table in the shade by the shop.

He'd come in as usual that morning, ordered his coffee and his morning goods. Catching my eye, you could see him calculating whether he could get away with pretending that yesterday hadn't happened.

'*Excusez-moi pour hier,*' he said at last. '*Il y a eu malentendu.*'

'Please don't worry sir,' I said piously, switching to English to underline the formality of the moment. 'It does not . . . regard me.'

'*Je vous remercie,*' he said with feeling. '*Alors . . . un grand crème et deux croissants aux amandes, s'il vous plait.*'

'*Pas de baguettes?*' I asked.

'*Non, merci,*' he said. '*Pas de baguettes.*' He looked at me gravely as he said this, as if we both knew that the time for baguettes had been and gone.

It was just a few minutes after that when former Mme B spotted him. My English was pretty good, but you didn't have to be fluent to get the gist.

She: 'What the fuck are you doing here?'

The girls: 'Dad!'

He: 'I can be here if I want to be.'

She: 'Fucking get away from us!'

The girls: 'Mum!'

He: 'Can't we please just talk?'

She: 'Can't you just leave us alone? How did you even find us?'

The girls: 'Mum!! Dad!!'

Twitchy Jogging Man (newly arrived on the scene): 'Are you OK, Tanya? Is he bothering you?'

He: 'Aaaaaaaaaaaaaaauuuuuuuuuuuuuuurrrrrghhhhhhhhhh-hhhhhhhhh!'

He stood and howled at her, eyes angry-red with tears. She sent the kids off to the beach with Twitchy Jogging Man and went off to find someone at reception 'in Security'. Good luck with that, I thought. The best you'll get is a couple of gangly eighteen-year olds in polo shirts and flip flops. Sure enough, Thierry and Jean-Luc, another life-guard, were soon seen striding self-importantly down towards us, flanking *le patron* himself. M Dubois was a slightly doddery seventy-some-thing, but he had the gravitas of ownership about him, and that was usually enough to dispel any tricky situation.

My Monsieur Brexit was led into the back of the beach shop, which happened to be the nearest spot where a bit of privacy could be had. M Dubois went in with him alone, and the two of them spoke in grave French undertones for a good twenty minutes. When they emerged, M Dubois shook his hand with great ceremony, and offered his condolences. After that, Thierry and Jean-Luc stood around awkwardly while the *Britannique* gathered his paper and his pastries, then escorted him to his one-man tent and his packing. On his way out, he came over to me where I still stood, by a rack of spinning windmills and sandcastle flags.

'*Merci pour tout, mademoiselle,*' he said gravely, and held out a hand.

'*Je vous en prie, monsieur,*' I said back, mechanically shaking the clammy palm.

When Thierry came back, he filled me in on the details, though of course Jeanette and I had pieced most of it together already. Monsieur Brexit and Tanya, his ex-wife, had split several months ago, for reasons unknown (though perhaps not impossible to guess at). She'd moved on, met someone else. He'd had a hard time accepting it was over, started following her around. He'd managed to track her down to this campsite, where he met her new boyfriend for the first time.

'Why did you always call him Monsieur Brexit, anyway?' asked Thierry. 'He told me several times in the shop he didn't even want to leave Europe.'

'I know,' I said. 'He just kept apologising for it.'

It seemed a good moment to say something else. 'By the way, Thierry, you should know that Magalie's already with someone.'

'No she's not,' he said crossly, and stalked off to Aquarobics.

FIRST-WORLD PROBLEMS

and then Middle One came in and said she was feeling sick and
you woke me up and asked me to move the bin nearer her as
she was going to puke again and I was grumpy and you said
you couldn't move because she was tucked under your arm
and then Charlie came in and started pumping everyone's
stomachs with his paws like he knew what was going on and
was trying to help and then Middle One *was* sick and I took
the bin to the bathroom and tried to slosh it all down the
shower but it got stuck and I had to try and push it all down
the plughole with my fingers and I complained about being
woken up and you said if I didn't want to be disturbed I
could sleep in the middle of the bed and I said it was no use
now I'd never get back to sleep and I made a big martyr
thing of going down at dawn and we both knew that even
though you'd got the bed you'd be the one that would have
to actually look after her while I just sat with my cuppa flicking through Twitter and I knew when you woke up we'd have
the usual passive-aggressive tussle about who would have to
stay at home with her and about work-life balance and who
has the harder time juggling stuff even though we both know
that my work really don't mind me working from home and
you had that training thing for your new job so really there

was no argument and I said that I'd had to fish out a load of tissue from the shower and you said are you sure the tissue wasn't in the bin already and that it wasn't you that actually tipped it in there in the first place and I was about to snap back at you but then I realised that this was actually a much more likely explanation especially as it was dark and I didn't have my glasses on and then Younger One came down and pretended to be sick so he could have a day off too and I had a long chat with him about Oldest One's molar coming in and he kept looking at my neck and asking when would they appear on her neck like mine and only then did I realise that he thought I was talking about moles and even Older One was in a goodish mood and then I realised again that I love you and we are happy and so many aren't

OUR SPECIAL WORDS
FOR THINGS

Anti-burst hose
Don't ask.

Bad fairy
A person who deliberately inflicts **bad medicine** (ie non-Fairy tablets) on their machine. Over time, this became your nickname for me whenever I'd done anything silly or naughty, such as overloading or giving in to my **self-storage delusion**. Or mixing up your meds or not realising that a pill organiser is an obvious **no-goer**.

Bad medicine
What you called the cheap tablets I'd buy when you weren't paying attention. You always reminded me that several top manufacturers recommend Fairy Platinum, and skimping a couple of quid on some cheap imitation would actually cost us more in the long run. 'Buy cheap, buy twice,' as you always liked to say. (Not to be confused with that other bad medicine, the stuff that made you bruise like a peach and made all your muscles go numb.)

Blocker
A person with a habit of stacking the machine so that the sprayer arms catch or the machine won't even shut properly. Yep, me again. (Did you know I sometimes did a bit of blocking on purpose, just to see your comedy angry face?) (I think you knew.) (I loved that face.)

Cycle rage
Your frustration on discovering that I had mistakenly set the machine going on Eco yet again. 'It washes less intensively and takes hours,' you said. 'And we just don't have the time.'

Handling the situation
(Something you were always better at than me.) Your name for the process of going through the cutlery tray and putting all the handles the right way up or down – blades down for knives (safety first), handles first for everything else (gets all the **spoonage** off).

Intervention
The unscheduled opening of the dishwasher door mid-cycle, usually to remedy a case of **nervous ticking** or to retrieve a utensil or container that has suddenly become essential to the cook. Should only ever be done as a last resort, you always said, because untold – though never fully explained – damage could apparently be done to the inner workings of the mechanism by the repetition of such emergency procedures. (Mind you, they saved you a couple of times.)

Kitchen cabinet syndrome
See **self-storage delusion**.

Kitchenware organisation and sanitation specialist (KOSS)
The title that you believed should be given to those rare elite

beings in the world who could stack a dishwasher as well as you. 'That's a bit of mouthful,' I said. 'Just think of me as your KOSS,' you said. 'Give me a kiss, my KOSS,' I said, and you did.

Last-minute Lulu
The kind of **bad fairy** who will spend 10 minutes rearranging the whole dishwasher just to squeeze in that one extra cup that they can't be bothered to wash, even though they will almost certainly be ruining the optimum stacking arrangement in the process. Yes, OK, me again.

Mouth-to-mouth
The practice, only to be used as a last resort, of trying to blow water through the tiny apertures in the dishwasher blade, so as to remove a stubborn bit of eggshell or congealed rice. You never know when that first aid training might come in handy.

Nervous ticking
The name for that noise you made every time the machine started emitting the sort of rhythmic clicking or scraping sound that could only be the result of a schoolgirl loading error. It would take every fibre of your will to resist the urge to stage an **intervention**. But you held on for as long as you could.

No-goer
Our term for any items that should never be put in the dishwasher, such as chopping boards, non-stick pans and bone china. You didn't like me putting my flip flops or plastic hairbrushes in, even though the internet said it was OK, but I think you were just jealous because my hair wasn't falling out. But you cheered up when I found out we could put your Macmillan baseball cap in there too.

Peak plenitude
A perfectly filled, optimally full load, ready for operation. Dishwasher Nirvana.

Phillys
Name given to the mysterious person who systematically over-fills the machine because they can't be bothered to wash up a few bits by hand. I vividly remember you sighing with dis-appointment as you opened the door and spied another selection of only partially washed crocks: 'I see Phyllis has been at it again . . .' The name derives, I assume, from the verb 'fill'. I'll never know for sure now.

Running on empty
A despairing phrase that describes any scenario involving the dishwasher running at less than **peak plenitude**.

Self-storage delusion
The heretical belief that the dishwasher is a mere cupboard (or **kitchen cabinet**) into which dirty stuff can be just shoved out of the way, to create a spurious impression of a spotless, decluttered kitchen. (Then again, I wouldn't have got through that week with all your family here otherwise. Had to buy a dozen extra mugs too: what else can people do at a time like that but drink more tea?)

Spoonage
A disparaging term for the gunk that is left on larger utensils such as wooden spoons, whisks and fish slices when they have been lazily arranged across the lateral racks above the upper tray in such a way as to have little chance of actually getting fully clean. (Though of course one should *never* put wooden spoons in a dishwasher, as you repeated ad nauseam.)

Stack attack
A dishwasher crime scene where everything has just been loaded willy-nilly, with no thought given to efficient use of space or cleansing optimisation.

Stackacious!
A high term of praise for a well-stacked machine, said when a **stack-check** was found to reveal no requirement for any remedial work. 'Wow! That was stackacious!' you sometimes used to say. (I'm glad something still gave you a thrill, in the last days.)

Stack-check
A favourite ritual of yours where you would review my attempt to fill the machine properly before it was switched on, and correct any obvious organisational inefficiencies. Regrettably your procedures in this regard, once so robust and relentless, slacked off considerably as time wore on. 'Stack-check please!' I'd call from the kitchen; '**Stackacious!**' you'd call weakly from the sofa. In the last days, you didn't even call back. But I like to think you still heard me, because once I came in and found you smiling. Your eyes were closed, but you were smiling.

Surgical procedures
Any of a range of remedial actions involving rolled-up sleeves and sump filter or circulating pump. Can rescue an apparently hopeless situation, for a time at least.

Wish-washer
A person who would kill to need to use their machine more often, now that they're only cooking for one.

Zanussi
The name I used to give to my imaginary lover. 'If you don't take your pills like a man, I'm calling Zanussi. He's waiting to

whisk me away, you know. Says he wants to sweep me up in his Whirlpool of hot love . . .' 'Zanussi wouldn't refuse his food like that.' It's funny, but I find I use our special names for things more than ever, now that *you*, of all people, are my imaginary lover.

Zeolite

The Siemens IQ500 machine uses zeolite in its drying process, a smart little mineral that can convert the moisture it absorbs into heat energy. This makes the machine especially good for hard-to-dry plastics and for making glassware shimmer.

*Farewell, my last and best friend, purveyor of **peak plenitude**. Farewell, my zeolite, you who made everything shimmer.*

HOTEL DU JACK

SATURDAY

Jack Ladd spent the first night of his family holiday doing shots at the bar with a few of the boys he'd met kite-surfing.

It had been a top day. The winds had been feisty but true, and now the six of them were quietly purring with that feeling of benign but hard-earned lassitude that follows a day of sun, sea and aerobic adventure.

A phone beeped.

Don't get too pissed for you know what, his wife texted. Sally was a couple of doors down, in their quaint little boutique beach view hotel, tucked up with their two daughters. No doubt watching *X Factor* or *The Voice* or some-such shite.

Jack grinned his full jackal grin, and generously passed the text around for all the lads to see.

'You lucky fuck,' said Paddy. 'My missus would be on sex-strike by now.' He mimicked a generic shrew voice: *What about me? What about the kids? Are you going to spend any time with us this week? I swear you'd rather be married to that surfboard than me!*

Jack held up his hand and effected an expert pause. 'Is she . . . *Belgian* then, mate?' he asked, and they all sniggered.

'Or maybe mate,' said Jack, peeling off his wetsuit top, balancing on the top rung of his barstool and giving each of his guns a wet kiss. 'Maybe she's the lucky fuck!'

The other lads cheered and cackled, louder this time. The bar was almost empty – indeed, with the as-yet-mild but unmistakably aggressive undercurrent of their exuberance, they had helped to empty it. Their noise had grown as they had taken possession of their territory.

But no one thought to disagree with Jack, or to laugh at his posturings. The fact was that – even half-cut and semi-slurring, as he was now – Jack was a physically compelling specimen, with veins that stood out on his forearms like cables and a six-pack as vehemently articulated as a lobster's tail.

He was the most ripped of the lot of them, the natural recipient of their unspoken deference. On a night like this, in among the chorus of guffaws and the comedy neck-holds, the increasingly explicit one-liners offered to passing females and the necking of flaming drinks that no one remembered ordering, they all got to bask a little in the reflected glory of Jack's effortless Jack-ness.

For they were men, all of them. And they were *magnificent*.

SUNDAY

Jack knew that a body like his came with certain responsibilities. Not to the wife so much, of course; she was lucky enough to have access all the time. (He'd done his best last night, but the details were hazy. He had a memory of Sally saying something like *Gerroff*, and pushing her feet against the wall to lever him out of the bed. When he'd finally woken up, he was wrapped in half a duvet on the carpet. His daughters, now absent, had placed two of their Little Live Pets on his chest for company. Frosty and Snuggles, at a guess.)

No, Jack mused to himself as he put his exquisite frame through a few pumps and rolls and crunches, his responsibility was more to the world at large. He was a bit like a singer with a miraculous voice. His was a gift to share. He understood that people *needed* to come up and squeeze his biceps and punch his washboard stomach – quite brazen about it too, they were, especially the ladies – and he gave freely of himself. He understood, because he had been like them once himself. He hadn't always been this buff, believe it or not, and he knew people needed to see that such perfection was possible.

Otherwise, what was there to hope for?

His body, as always, felt tip-top. One of the perks of working your sweet self as hard as he did was a miraculous ability to bounce back from a heavy night or three. His head, however, was something else. And looking at the empty en-suite, the ruffled kids' beds and the radio-alarm beeping a reproachful 11.47am, he sensed a certain disapproval in the air. He had failed to show Sally some decent Jack-love. He had left her to deal with the kids on her own on the first day of the very *family* holiday, he could hear her saying, that they had both agreed they so badly needed. The girls had probably been up since six.

There was more. His unorthodox sleeping position had left him with a nagging strain in his right trap, which if he wasn't careful could hamper his holiday workout routine significantly. And in his pissed-up state he had allowed himself to eat half a plateful of nachos smothered in melted cheese. He dreaded to think of the extra load of empty calories he'd have to work off, not to mention the impact on muscle growth of so much unrefined shite. *What was he thinking?*

But even that was not all. For, with the sort of jolt of panic that must accompany the first irrefutable sign of madness, Jack realised that he had not today as yet given a single thought . . . to his *hair*.

He rushed to the bathroom, and began to tease and smooth his neglected locks in the mirror's fond gaze. All was not lost, for there were products a-plenty in the dedicated sponge bag he'd insisted on packing separately. Already a strategy was forming in his mind: a look that would set off his high forehead to advantage but also be robust enough for a day's salt air and hardcore watersport. A touch of bedhead, of course, but tempered with something more architectural, a compelling synergy of sprawl and structure.

'I don't know how you can spend so much time on it every day,' Sally always mocked. 'All you do is just scrunch it all up and slather in that horrible gel stuff.' He smiled. He liked a woman who gave as good as she got. She was the mother of his children, so he would never diss her, but sometimes her humour got very close to the bone.

With thoughts like these, then, Jack's day began to arrange itself. Shower, shampoo, shave, high-carb brunch with a protein shake. Hair. Family time on the beach. Track down the boys later. Maybe get the boat out, or take up Billy's offer of some jet skis. But first things first.

It was while he was on the loo that Jack first spotted it, tucked on a little shelf of books and magazines strategically placed for browsing on the crapper. A paperback book in a dullish magnolia colour. On the front, a picture of a woman sitting in an armchair, in a dress that even his great aunt (if he had one) would have thought a bit frumpish. Next to her stood a little table, and on it, a couple of limp flowers in a vase. The woman's head was tilted wearily away from the reader, so that you could only really see her hair, a long limp curtain of mousiness that was obviously a lifelong stranger to product and styling alike. The armchair sat in front of a massive window, but you couldn't really see out of it because there was a massive beige curtain in front. There was obviously a bit of a breeze outside, because the curtain was billowing up a bit at the bottom, offering a teasing glimpse of balcony and a tiny triangle of blue, presumably sea.

It was, Jack thought, probably the dullest book cover he had ever seen. It was as if the designer had set himself – or herself, it could have been a lady – the challenge of creating the least memorable cover image ever. It was the sort of book cover that seemed designed to draw your attention only to the curtains. This was a mistake in Jack's view, because although the woman looked boring and her face was hidden, she was at least *a person*; the drapes, meanwhile, were dowdy and yellow looking, they weren't even top-of-the-range as far as he could see.

Jack was a big reader. He was a completist. He had read all of Lee Child, some of them two or three times, and he was closing in on similar conquests of both Nesbo and Larsson. Nor was he a stranger to the classics: he had read widely among the greats, notably Sheldon, King, Ludlum and Herbert. If you didn't remember where you were when you read *that* scene in *The Fog* then, to Jack's mind, you didn't know literature. (Hint: garden shears, cocks chopped off etc.)

He flipped the book, which was called something he instantly forgot, and saw it was written by one Angela Brocker, or something. He read the blurb:

'I never knew about this place while he was alive. But now – thanks to him of all people – I have a chance to find myself at last.'

Three years after the demise of her demanding husband Victor, Patricia Porlock is living in modest but comfortable seclusion in a one-bedroom pied-a-terre in Chelsea that she only found out about from his will.

Now, with the freedom to put her own needs first at last, Patricia begins to reflect on a difficult marriage and the sacrifices she made to keep it afloat.

But into this life of calm contemplation enter three unwelcome visitors, whose claims on Patricia's past, present and future threaten in their different ways to undermine all her hard-earned equilibrium . . .

'*Jesus H*,' Jack said to himself. He turned to the first page. It began:

'I think after all I *shall* have some broccoli,' said Patricia Porlock to the young waitress, noticing as she did so a sensation of great pleasure sweeping through her.

Jack threw the book at the floor and applied himself to his movement.

'Here you go – she's all yours!' said Sally sharply, as soon as Jack had made his way over the sands to where she was sitting with the girls, in what was – he noticed with a stab of irritation – exactly the same spot as yesterday. *Boring!*

She shoved one of the twins into his hastily outstretched arms, and said: 'I'm going for a coffee.' She stalked off pointedly, or at least as pointedly as the deep sand would allow. As he knew from his attempted jog yesterday – great resistance training, sand on bare feet, of course – it was hard to do much on this surface except a sort of clownish waddle.

He looked at the little girl. He was pretty sure it was Abby. Abby had the longer hair. Or she did have. Didn't Sally just get them both a trim, though? She should have given them different looks. She should have asked him, come to that, he knew a lot about hair. He could ask his daughter who she was, of course, but Sally had told him to stop doing this – 'You'll give her a complex, Jack!' Quick as a flash, he'd replied: 'Which one?'

Abby (probably) wanted to get into her swimsuit but somehow the Velcro strap of one of her sandals had got caught up in her pink jogging bottoms. She'd fallen flat on her face, and sand was now plastered on all the areas she had painstakingly pre-coated with chocolate ice cream. Jack disentangled his daughter, clumsily cleaned her off with some wipes, and began rummaging around in Sally's day-bag for her next outfit. Tilly (probably), her twin sister, was already dressed in her sunsuit, which was ideal for sand *or* sea.

These sunsuits were great outfits, Jack thought appraisingly, sort of somewhere between a lycra base layer and a light wetsuit. He wondered if you could get a men's version and, if so, whether it would fit him. It'd be a great sculpted look, obviously, only his biceps were so broad he sometimes struggled to squeeze into the sleeves of such things.

There followed about half an hour of desultory castle-building, and several stop-start games of catch with his Nerf Vortex Mega Howler (or 'that stupid whistling rugby ball thing with the long tail', as Sally ignorantly called it). Then Jack took to whirling the girls through the tide, threatening to dunk them in head first as they screamed in delighted horror. Quite a good upper-body workout, this, especially as they were a decent weight now. And then, with a feeling of intense relief, Jack spotted that Sally was on her way back. She'd bought him a cappuccino and a paper. The mood, he sensed, had lifted.

'So . . . Did you have nice time with the lads last night? Not keeping you up, were we?' Her face was mock-resentful, with that underlying twinkle of mischief he loved about her.

'I'm sorry love. Got a bit carried away.' He grabbed a well-pedicured foot as she dug a sharp row of pretty toes into his thigh. She looked him frankly in the eyes. He thought: She doesn't know whether to punch me or fuck me. He took a punt and said: 'You are really doing it for me right now, babe.'

'Bastard,' she said, driving her foot into him again. *Oh yes*, he thought. Smashed it. Jack's done it again. Later he would re-acquaint her with Little Jack. The Jackster. Jack in the Box. Jack, son of Jack. The Jackatola. Jack the JackRabbit. Jack-in-the-Sack. The Jackal. Mr JackHammer. Jumping Jack Flash. (They had lots of names for it.) (Well, he did.)

He took her foot and he kissed it. She was always at her sexiest when she was about to forgive him. (She was often at her sexiest.)

Then he reached for his Michael Phelps XCEED Titanium Mirror racing goggles.

'What you doing?' she said.

'Just going for a quick dip,' he said. 'Clear my head a bit.'

'OK,' she relented. 'But don't leave me with the girls all afternoon.'

'Course not,' he said, leaning over and rewarding her with a lingering kiss on the lips.

He stood, arched his back, rolled his shoulders, adjusted his goggles, stretched his trunk, tightened his trunks. People were looking at him, he could sense it. He was used to it, and he completely got it – he was so shredded, it was almost obscene. Coming across a body like his in the course of a normal day was a scandal to the senses, he knew, a bit like a nipple popping out in church, or the sudden appearance of an engorged bell-end in a court of law.

I'd probably be gawking right now too, mused Jack, if *I* saw me for the first time. Course I would.

He strode to the water's edge, looked out dramatically over the horizon, bent down and applied a few splashes of seawater to his dramatic torso.

'Play with me, Daddy!' said Abby – it was probably Abby – whom he hadn't spotted was filling her bucket with wet sand nearby.

'Won't be a sec, love,' he smiled. 'Daddy just do a quick

swim.' He looked over at Sally, caught her eye, and very quickly did the following: he pointed at Abby and then back to Sally and then at Abby again, pulled down one of his eyes, and then pointed at Sally again. Then he repeated the whole thing again, much quicker. This was all of course international parent code for: 'All yours now, babe. I'm signing off.'

Now he turned to the sea and, without looking back again, and certainly without flinching for an instant, he walked straight out into the briskly chilly waves, like a modern god from an after-shave ad. And then, when he could walk no more, he swam. Out and out he swam with his effortless technique, gloriously streamlined, straight as a torpedo. Out and out he swam, in his restless quest for Peak Condition.

Twisting expertly over on to his back for a scheduled resting pause, Jack looked back across the water at the beach. One of the twins was looking up at her mum, he saw, shoulders hunched and hands tucked over her groin, as if squaring up to a free-kick. Sally, meanwhile, was holding her daughter at arm's length; she was also holding her nose, while looking around for something. Then, for a second, Sally seemed to be looking for him, scanning the sea with a hand over her eyes. He waved. Sally was mouthing something back, but he didn't quite catch it.

MONDAY

Fucking shrimps. Never eat the *fucking shrimps*. When would he ever learn?

It was 3.23am and Jack was lying on the cold, tiled floor of the en-suite, leaking miserably from both ends.

After taking the girls for a burger, he and Sally had got them off to sleep, ordered some room service and made up their own dessert.

Barely had his heart returned to resting rate when the first cramps began. It was just little stomach twinges at first, but then came the waves of nausea. These developed into an ominous feeling that a terrible storm was threatening the ocean of fluid in his stomach. He felt an overwhelming queasiness that might have made a weaker man question the very meaning of life. The only way out was through, Jack knew, but even he quailed before the task.

He lay moaning into the small hours, trying to trick his body into sleep. In the end, he rose and took up the position: head over porcelain, fingers down throat. His first few attempts did nothing to dispel the nauseous dread – if anything, they made it worse. He lay back on the bathroom floor, weak and helpless, quietly scandalised that Sally was able to sleep through the dark night of his despair. (Not only sleep, in fact; she was actually snoring sarcastically.) He wouldn't wake her, though; even in his enfeebled state, he was smarter than that. To endure this plight alone would gain him serious credit, credit he could usefully cash in later in the week.

One full waking nightmare later, as the dawn-light began to steal through the en-suite window, Jack was aware at last that he could actually move an arm or leg without instantly retching. He crawled back to bed, and only when he got there did he find that he was clutching the book that had lain by his head throughout his ordeal, the magnolia-coloured curtain book whose title he still couldn't remember.

He spent most of that day under the duvet. When the kids had come in and woken them up at 6.04am, he'd told them all about the miseries of the night before. He didn't need to lay it on thick; indeed, he found that the less he said, the more sympathetic and compassionate they became. 'It must have been awful,' said Sally, feelingly. 'I mean, just look at your *hair*.' (So she *did* get him, after all!)

After breakfast – nothing for him, of course – Sally had taken the girls off to the beach, and promised to leave him alone to recover. So now it was just him and his mobile. He texted Paddy and a couple of the others from the bar – wakeboarding was on the agenda for later, which he might have to pass on. But he missed the boys, missed their unquestioning approval of him. He got them to sign him up for tomorrow's cave-dive, whatever that was.

Jack worked on the London commodities desk of an Asian merchant bank. The work was mental, and his colleagues were all fuckwits. Here was an email now from 'Geordie'. Though 'Geordie' – one of Jack's bitterest rivals, commission wise – had a funny northern accent, he got very upset trying to explain to people that he didn't actually come from Newcastle or anywhere near it. Once the boys saw how much this bugged him, of course, 'Geordie' became his nickname for life.

This was probably a better nickname than 'T-Shirt', mind you, which had been given to the lad – Simon, was it? Jack couldn't even remember his real name now – who had once turned up for work in a Prada suit and a Paul Smith shirt – *with a T-shirt underneath it.* This was such a hideous faux pas, he'd been known as 'T-Shirt' ever since, even though – as he'd recently tried to point out – the incident had taken place over seven years ago. To which Jack and the others had said, as one: 'Fuck off, T-Shirt.'

Anyway here was a message now, from 'Geordie', sent to Jack and cc-ed to the rest of his male colleagues. Subject line: 'You've been replaced with a real muppet.' The message read: 'Hi Jack, hope you're having a lovely time. Just thought you'd want to know, in your absence, we've found a proper muppet to do your job . . . (see attached). And guess what? The numbers are up . . . !!!'

Jack clicked on the attachment. It was a picture of a large cuddly Kermit, who had been posed sitting at Jack's very own desk, typing at his very own keyboard with one furry green hand (paw?), and dipping his other green hand (or paw) into a massive bucket of USN Anabolic Nitro-X. Jack's very own bucket of the specialist supplement, in fact, which he had anecdotally proven to his own satisfaction did indeed, as claimed, speed up muscle recovery between sets of reps.

Classic bantz. Weakly, Jack texted back: 'Fuck off racists', and threw his phone down on the duvet. He felt so drained and so bored that he picked up the magnolia curtain book again.

It was like no other book that Jack had ever read.

For a start, there was a fuck of a lot about meals. Huge amounts of the text were devoted to accounts of people ringing each other up to see if they wanted to come to lunch. He lost track of how many pages were spent on descriptions of tea and cakes being ordered in the restaurants of high-end department stores. The main character Patricia's relationship with her fishmonger, an extrovert Frenchman called Grégoire, was given special attention throughout, even though there was no indication that the pair had ever fucked or fought or even knew each other very well. He didn't even give her free fish.

Then there was a load of stuff about feelings. The pages were full of descriptions of every little thing that happened to Patricia, and of how each thing made her *feel*. Delight at being able to declutter* all the surfaces in the kitchen at last. Anxiety about her ageing mum's appetite (she'd stopped eating the pickled fruit Patricia always made for her). Self-consciousness in the hairdresser's at trying out a new look (*you what?*). Irritation at Gordon, the bumbling old flame who comes

---

* Although 'declutter', as Jack would learn later (p159) was not a word that Patricia would ever use. 'It's like upcycling,' Patricia mused to herself in Habitat later that morning. 'One sees the benefits and one applauds the concept. It's just not the way one would choose to put it.'

sniffing around the flat once he finds out Patricia's a widow, when all she wants is a bit of peace and quiet. (Gordon must be the first of the three unwelcome visitors, Jack reckoned, and even though he was some kind of ex, it didn't even seem as if he'd ever had sex with Patricia either. No one fucked in fact; it was a book that didn't seem to have heard of sex.)

Most of the stuff that Patricia felt was pointless, banal, tedious, domestic. But that didn't matter. If she felt it – in it went.

Above all, though, Patricia rambled on about her dead hubby Victor. Why she did this, Jack could not fathom, because he was obviously a miserable old fuck and she was well shot of him. He was a big portly man, who had made loads of money in the eighties and didn't really ever listen to anything she said. He had some job in finance which she never understood and he never really tried to explain to her. (The details were sketchy but to Jack it sounded like some sort of due diligence role on the private equity side.) Her job was mostly to look pretty and put on nice dinners when he brought clients round. Between the lines, Jack sensed that Patricia was secretly over the moon that he'd snuffed it, but she didn't go on about what a cock he was, or how made up she was to get her hands on his cash, or anything like that. No, mostly she just seemed chuffed to have a free run of the cookbooks for once:

> She could change her mind as often as she liked now, she said to herself, and she could conjure up all the things she'd always liked that Victor hadn't – things she'd trained herself not to miss over so many years. Creamed kale? Dauphinoise potatoes? Blanched asparagus with hand-dived scallops in a caviar sauce? Well, why not? A whole vista of delightful new possibilities spread out before her mind's eye. And she felt only the mildest pang of guilt that she owed the indulgence of such gastronomic fantasies to the passing of her fastidious life-mate.

Jack had reached page 71 of the book, and still he had yet to encounter a single action scene. Not only was there was no sex. There was no violence. No crime or criminals. No high-tech gadgetry. No geopolitical shenanigans, no money laundering, no gangland hits. No car chases or death threats or bent coppers. No suspense even – unless you could work up some curiosity about what side dish she might finally order with her lamb cutlets.

There were, however, two pages devoted to a phone call about a recipe for a Victoria sponge, plus a lengthy chat about sea bream, and six paragraphs on Gordon's inability to make a decent pot of coffee, and what that said about him.

True to its cover, there was a decent section – about a page and a half – on Patricia's curtains. Victor had liked them, but she thought on reflection that they weren't really her. There was a good chance she might change the curtains, Jack reckoned, before the book was out.

All in all, then, it was a book about nothing. Yet somehow Jack was already over a third of the way through it.

TUESDAY

Jack had never cave-dived before, but he had done a fair few other outdoor activities of the extreme, high-adrenaline variety. He had bungee-jumped and parascended and zip-wired down mountain valleys. He had bouldered and canyoned and zorbed with the best of them.

Now he stood outside their holiday cottage, waiting for Paddy's beach camper to pick him up. He made good use of the time with a few ultra-speed turns on his Buddy Lee Aero Speed Jump Rope, voted 'the smoothest, fastest, and best-balanced rope, period' by none other than *Men's Health* magazine, the world's leading anti-fat Bible.

'You ever cave-*died* before then, mate?' said Paddy. 'Sorry, I meant cave-*dived*.'

The rest of the lads – a couple from Saturday night, plus a few more that Jack had never met – guffawed appreciatively, and Jack did his best to as well.

'Nah.'

'Well, it's been nice knowing you, mate,' said the one called 'Zippy', and they all guffawed again.

Jack – who until this moment had forgotten that he was scared of only two things in the world, sharks and confined spaces – felt an odd sensation. He couldn't quite put his finger on it, but if pushed to give it a name, he might call it *dread*, perhaps. Or even *fear*. Or even, and this was just a wild guesstimate, maybe *abject terror at the prospect of imminent death*.

And what was worse, the lads could sense it. They could smell it. They may have deferred to Jack at the height of his boozy powers, with biceps glistening and women throwing themselves at him, but that only made them enjoy his obvious discomfort all the more now.

'Whatever you do, don't shit yourself in the water,' the one called 'Nitro' was saying now to the one called 'Spum'. 'That'll bring the sharks in quicker than blood.'

'I thought there weren't any serious sharks in these waters,' said Jack, much too quickly.

'Oh they'll come in from miles for a bit of anal,' said the one called 'Spum'. 'Fresh squit really does it for them.'

How would Patricia Porlock deal with this situation? Jack found himself thinking. Well, for starters, she'd never get into this fucking situation. About the most daring thing she did in the whole magnolia curtain book was to go on the Northern line – and even then she brought hand gel.

Gordon might have wanted her to do a few more risqué things, of course. But it wasn't the thought of sleeping with Gordon that put Patricia off, at least not in Jack's view. Gordon, after all, was actually quite a handsome chap in a rather old-fashioned sort of way, a man of slacks and bow ties

and sensible slip-ons who still thought tashes were accept-
able. (Patricia said little about his hair but, judging by his
outfits, Jack could only imagine the worst.)

No, the problem with Gordon was that he was lonely. He
just wanted someone kind and nice-looking to keep him
company on his weekend breaks to cathedral cities, and to
make nice meals for him of an evening. He was a lazy
sponger of Patricia's time, that was all he was, who didn't get
that Patricia actually liked being on her own. For her, being
alone meant being *free*.

What was it he'd said to her?

'Isn't it something to have an agreeable companion
with whom to share the nicer things in life, Patricia, even –
or especially – at our age?'

Jack had been terrified she'd give in to him. She was vulnerable, after all, not long a widow. And for all her resolutions,
having a bloke around had its advantages.

But no, she was having none of it. She put down her
cream scone, looked him in the eye, and said:

'It all depends on one's view of what constitute "the
nicer things", I suppose .'

Fucking take *that*, Gordon, you dull fuck. He was clearly
winded, bouncing off the ropes, but – give him credit – he
had another crack.

'Why – culture, the sights, a walk in the woods . . .' said
Gordon, looking off into some imaginary distance. 'A
Mozart concerto. A crisp glass of Chardonnay. Sunset on
a balcony by the sea. Surely everyone finds these things
agreeable?'

Quick as a flash, she came right back at him.

'I always think "agreeable" is such an *insipid* sort of a
word, don't you?' smiled Patricia, as if to herself. Gordon
looked thoughtfully at his teacake.

Smack. It was fucking brutal. Gordon was down and he was
out. The ref stepped in, closely followed by the paramedics,
and Gordon was no more.

'All right Jack, mate?' said the one called 'Pogo', snapping
Jack out of his reverie.

'Course.'

'Remember, mate: diving isn't dangerous.'

'I know.'

'Only drowning is.'

Jack put down his imaginary cream scone. He said: 'Fuck
off, jizz-chops.'

Roars all round from the van.

The boat that was to take them out to the cave-dive site was
called *The Marabar.* The smell of petrol was overpowering.
That and the rocking from the choppy water quickly got Jack
feeling queasy all over again.

'See this dial here,' said the one called 'Termite'. 'This
basically tells you how deep they'll find your body.'

Patricia Porlock had some tough situations to face too,
Jack recalled, now that she was on her own. Although Victor
clearly didn't know one end of a nutmeg grater from
another, he had at least been on hand to do some of the
obvious (or traditional) blokey stuff. He always handled all
their investments, of course, and Patricia has a terrible time
trying to deal with her new financial adviser, a dodgy plum-
voiced geezer recommended to her by Gordon.

When Patricia tries to diversify some of her stock into more secure instruments (and to Jack's mind this makes perfect sense as a strategy, portfolio wise, given her as-yet-limited understanding of the markets), her new adviser tells her that she is 'possessed of an appetite to risk that is unhealthily conservative'. The patronising fuck. Poor Patricia fled the intimidatingly grand Mayfair office, biting back her tears.

But she'd held out for what she wanted, and she'd got it. Good for her.

Victor had also taken charge of anything to do with the car, from the annual service to the topping-up of the screen-wash. This spelled new challenges for his widow too, of course, and there was a heart-rending scene where Patricia had to take their car into a garage to find out how to check the tyres have enough air in them. The mechanics – all 'orrible oafish grease-monkeys of course – were merciless in their mockery of her ignorance.

'Don't you have an old man to sort this stuff out for you, love?' said one. With terrible dignity, Patricia refused to play the widow card. 'I wish to learn these things for myself,' was all she said.

To add insult to injury, the car Patricia inherits from Victor is a big clunky S-Class Merc that is not remotely suited to her needs – and he never even used to let her get behind the wheel anyway, which makes her even more of an anxious driver now. Jack personally felt she would be much better off with something like a Hyundai i10, or even a Suzuki Ignis, though in truth she wasn't really much one for the driving at all, and in most of the book she makes do with cabs and the occasional bus.

In fact, the only time she really got the car out was when the second of her visitors, Ivy, a young niece of Victor's, insisted on being picked up from Heathrow with all her bags.

Ivy was just back from a gap year in Australia and now – it quickly transpired – expected Patricia to put her up at her place indefinitely while she worked out what she wanted to do with her life. Ivy was very definitely unwelcome visitor #2.

Two hours later, they were back in the boat. Jack was alive, and for this he was tearfully grateful. One of the few good things of being underwater, covered in a massive mask, clinging on for dear life in a dark vertical tunnel with no way out but forwards through excruciatingly narrow passages of cold, black, shark-infested sea, was that the other lads couldn't really see all the expressions of panic and horror and the pleas for divine mercy that he'd put his face through while they explored the cave.

'Cave', indeed, was a rather *insipid* word for the thing they'd just explored. For a start the only way into it involved a twenty-foot leap of faith, straight down into a 2p coin-sized opening surrounded by rocky spikes, any one of which could surely paralyse or castrate a man.

Then it was a matter of going down some more, down and down into ever darker and narrower spaces, with just the quickly-fading beams of their head-lamps for visibility. (Jack hadn't realised that what they were doing was also known as 'underwater pot-holing'.) And all the while, every secret fibre of him was screaming to make this whole experience stop, to make it go away, to fill his companions' minds as one with the sudden urge to turn back and head for the surface. Only now, they were in spaces so confined that for most of them – and especially for Jack, with his big stupid, pumped-up physique – turning back had actually become a physical impossibility. The only way out – and this was a truth Jack felt he had never really understood before, even though he said it to himself every time he was faced with the bodybuilder's *abyss*, that gaping void between the work that needed to be done and the actual doing of that work – the only way out was *through*.

'Well done, mate, you made it,' the one called 'Nitro' was saying to Jack, back at the bar.

Jack, who as recently as forty minutes ago had assumed that he was on the verge of a hideous death, was on his third tequila slammer already.

'Yup.'

'Bit too much for you, in there, was it, mate? Couldn't take the heat?'

As Jack took in the insidious sneering mugs of the ones called 'Nitro' and 'Pogo' and 'Zippy' and 'Spum' and 'Termite' – all eager to exploit his weakness, to expose the inner weed, the weeny balls, of the big bloated muscle-man – a stab of hostility flashed across his face. I could take you all now, it said, crush your stupid little heads together between my pecs. The others saw the look too, and they tensed for a confrontation; now at last, the day was heading for its consummation.

But then Jack's face changed, morphing into an expression none of the lads recognised and that he himself wouldn't have had a word for.

'Can I be absolutely frank with you?' said Jack amicably to the ones called 'Nitro' and 'Pogo'. 'I genuinely believed that I was about to meet my maker down there. I don't think I've ever actually been as frightened as that in my entire life. The only vaguely comparable experience was when they thought my twin daughters had meningitis, just after they were born. And to anyone who can enjoy such an audacious activity, one that for me, will always be associated with memories of the utmost terror, I take off my hat. I really do.'

His voice broke as he finished, and he shed a few silent tears. No one said anything. No one knew where to look. Everyone took a big drink.

'And now,' said Jack. 'Who'd like to see my cock?'

212

WEDNESDAY

Next day Jack woke early, feeling wonderfully restored to his old vibrant self. He decided to get out before breakfast for a light jog. The girls woke up as he banged about the room trying to select the best footwear for his run and searching for his new Apple Watch Nike+ Sports Band. Sally looked up at him blearily, a girl snuggled up on each side of her.

'Here Abby, Tilly!' he said on a sudden whim. (He said their names very fast so they wouldn't notice he couldn't quite tell them apart in the semi-darkness of the bedroom.)

'Yes, Daddy?' They looked up at him, eyes wide with innocent expectation, and also – he noticed, with a pang – a hint of surprise.

'Why don't you come out jogging with Daddy?'

'Yay!' they shouted as one.

'Yeah, let's do this! Go and get your clothes on then, girls! I expect your mum could do with a lie-in.'

The girls ran off as one to their room, where they could be heard rummaging through their bags and giggling loudly. Sally looked both grateful and gobsmacked. She looked, in fact, as if she expected him to announce that he was only joking.

'What's brought this on?' she said at last, as he headed for the door with his daughters in tow.

'I'm sure you could do with a moment's respite,' he said. 'I imagine the last few days have afforded you no little enervation.'

Even in her current state of muzzily grateful goodwill, Sally couldn't help emitting a derisive snort. 'Do you even know what "enervation" means?' she called out after him.

Outside their bedroom, he paused, and looked hard at the door he'd just closed. 'No,' he thought to himself, perplexed. 'I really don't.'

*

Jogging was obviously out of the question with two four-year-olds, but Jack found that the girls had great fun trying to mimic his morning routine of stretches and squats and tucks and shuffles. It was basically a mid-intensity beach circuit of his own devising, and he couldn't help smiling at the high-intensity expressions and exaggeratedly violent jerks of his daughters' attempts to copy him. He thought: Is this what I look like?

'Daddy,' said Abby, after about five minutes. (It was probably Abby.) 'Why are you always doing these funny exercises?'

'Gotta keep in shape, love. Keeps you fit and healthy.'

'But Daddy,' Abby persisted. (Probably Abby.) 'You already are in shape.'

'Yes, and what about Mummy?' said Tilly. (Probably Tilly.) 'She doesn't do all this funny stuff: Does that mean she isn't fit and healthy?'

'Course not, love!' he replied, careful not to refer to either daughter by name. 'She does fitness stuff too.' (In point of fact, Jack considered Sally's exercise choices dangerously skewed towards cardio-aerobic at the expense of core and tone, but this was not the moment to say so.)

'Yes but . . .'

'What, sweetie?'

'She doesn't do it all the time, like you.'

'Yes Daddy,' said maybe-Abby echoing maybe-Tilly. 'Why do *you* have to do it all the time?'

He stopped in mid shoulder-roll. A young seagull had begun pecking insolently at the tag of his Speedo Deluxe Ventilator Beach Bag. (He hated the juvenile gulls – they were like human teenagers. Lairy, lanky fuckers, bigger than the adults somehow, not afraid of anything. Always egging each other on.)

Out at sea, a ferry inched its way across the horizon.

Jack threw down his original, authentic 28olb Captains of Crush professional hand grippers, engineered from precision materials and widely considered the gold standard for building and testing grip strength.

'Who wants a fry-up?'

'Yay!'

'I'll text Mummy and tell her to meet us in the Italian caff.'

Fifteen minutes later, the four of them were happily squeezed into a booth around a plastic table in Giordano's.

Sally said, 'Do you want the beans or the mushrooms, Abby?'

Abby – for it had to be her – replied: 'I just can't decide, Mummy. It's all so yummy!!'

Jack looked up from his plate of eggs and chips, and made them laugh with his frothy moustache from the cappuccino he'd been hoovering up noisily.

'Do you know? In all the time I've known you,' said Sally wonderingly, 'this is the first time you've ever had chocolate on your coffee. Or frothy milk, come to that.'

'Mummy?' It was Abby again, awaiting the food umpire's decision. Sally looked at Jack.

He smiled indulgently at his eldest daughter. (Eldest by thirty-four minutes, he recalled.)

'You must have *both*, Abby, my dear,' he said.

'Are you sure?' said Sally.

'Why yes,' said Jack. 'One must relish those rare moments when life does not force us to renounce one pleasure for another.'

Back at the holiday home, Sally returned Jack's favour of early-morning childcare by running him a bath.

He poured in some bubbles and folded up his frame into the narrow Victorian tub as best he could. He kept his hands dry and clear of the water so he could read while he soaked.

Things in the magnolia curtain book had got very tense indeed. Victor's niece, Ivy, was basically taking the piss.

Coming home at all hours of the night – sometimes with a random bloke in tow; never saying where she'd be or what she was doing; never offering to help out with the shopping or the housework, let alone pay any rent. She treated Patricia's place like a bloody hotel. Worse, she was quietly sarcastic about her host's dress sense, decor and even her lifestyle. 'Sometimes, I think your curtains lead a more glamorous life than you do, auntie!' snarked Ivy at the end of one particularly tense exchange.

It was incredible, really, how it all came back to the curtains.

Ivy was basically one of life's takers. If you put your hand out to help her, she'd bite your arm off. In many ways she was far worse than Gordon, who at least paid his way and seemed to actually like Patricia. Gordon knew to withdraw when his offer was turned down. Ivy, on the other hand, seemed to quietly despise Patricia, yet showed no signs of ever moving on. Not so long as she had this meal-ticket on tap.

'*Change the fucking locks on her, Patricia!*' hissed Jack at the book. Here she was, just settling into a life on her own terms for once, and this streaky little millennial leech was ruining it all. And Patricia, she was just letting it happen!

When Victor had bequeathed her the flat, she wondered, had he intended her to use it for the purpose of playing house to Ivy? Perhaps, perhaps not. But even if not, the property had been a gift so miraculously suited to her present needs – needs which, once their own house had been sold, were not so much economical as emotional, or even, in some small way, spiritual – that it seemed ungrateful, churlish even, to refuse to share the benefits with another in need. And this had to be especially so in the case of Ivy who was, after all, Victor's own flesh and blood.

You are way too nice, girl, Jack thought again, splashing the frothy bathwater in exasperation.

But even someone as decorous and patient and by-the-book as Patricia has her limits. One morning, after waking to find that Ivy has left smeggy kebab wrappings all over Patricia's lovely sofa, and trodden fag-ash into her brand-new carpet, Patricia is moved to act at last. (The intrusion of so vulgar a thing as a chicken doner into Patricia's exquisite world struck Jack as an especially crude sacrilege.) But even now, pushed to the limit, Patricia's essential classiness shone through. Did she scream or shout? Did she change the locks, as Jack had urged? Did she kick Ivy out on her arse? Did she pluck a few pubes and serve them up in a ham sandwich, as Jack had once done to Geordie?

Oh no. She got out her Nile blue correspondence cards from Smythson of Bond Street, unleashed the old Mont Blanc Bohème fountain pen (a present from Victor on the occasion of their twentieth wedding anniversary, which was also her fifty-fourth birthday), and she wrote a letter.

Darling Ivy

It's been such a pleasure having you to stay these past few weeks. I have very much enjoyed getting to know you better and, in so doing, extending my acquaintance with a side of Victor's family of which, before your coming, I had been regrettably ignorant. Together we have shared several happy moments, forged several fond memories. ['Several!' squawked Jack in the bath. 'You are a *bad-ass*, Patricia babe!'] But now alas, I fear the time has come for us to go our separate ways . . .

The note went on to explain that certain unexpected financial constraints meant that Patricia would soon be forced to place the property on the market, prior to which she felt it necessary to undertake 'extensive renovations to fabric and decor, some of which have been suggested to me by your own fine judgements in these matters'. *Boom! Check out the sarcasm on that!* But Patricia wouldn't be leaving Ivy in the lurch, of course, oh no.

> I do so regret the inconvenience that this upheaval will inevitably cause to your plans, and am resolved to do everything in my power to assist you. I have this morning drafted a note to your grandmother, down in Heretic's Fork. If the rural life suits you, I am sure that Josephina will be delighted to host you for a decent interval . . .

Yes baby. Oh yes. You do it so right! whispered Jack to himself. Josephina, notoriously, lived alone with a menagerie of random beasts on a smallholding somewhere in deepest Wiltshire. She famously preferred animals to humans, and the one time Patricia had stayed there, she had to shield her dinner from a menacing horde of manky, toothless cats, and had woken up the next morning to find a rheumatic rescue goat licking her feet. As Victor said: 'Even her teapot smells of dog!'

All this, of course, added up to a hint that even Ivy could not fail to take. There were no financial troubles, they both knew that, and Patricia wasn't going anywhere. But if Ivy was going to trash Patricia's flat, both by her words and her actions, then she would have to sling her hook. Not that there was any need for unpleasantness. Patricia's delicate note, delivered in her classic hand, swathed in a signature Smythson tissue-lined envelope, gave them both an elegant out. Patricia had done right by Ivy and by Victor in all this, done more than right. But now, Ivy could just fuck right off. And she did.

I just love the way you do things Patricia, said Jack to the book. He was on page 147 of 212, and already he felt a terrible sense of grief to come at the prospect of reaching the book's end.

When, ten minutes later, Jack emerged in search of his styling putty, he was met at the bathroom door by a furious-looking Sally. The mood had clearly changed, and quite radically.

'How fucking dare you have phone sex in our holiday home?? The girls keep asking me who Daddy's talking to in the bathroom, you fucking sleazebag.' He held up a hand but she slapped it away. 'And who the fuck is Patricia?' she snarled.

THURSDAY

It had been harder than he expected to explain to Sally the nature of her misunderstanding. Sally was actually quite ready to be convinced that he hadn't been sexting another woman; whether she thought he was capable of this, he wasn't sure, but she certainly thought that if he was going to do the dirty on her he'd be more subtle about it.

The bit that really stretched her credulity, however, was the idea that Jack was hooked on a story by someone like Angela Brocker. She spent much of the afternoon flicking through his magnolia curtain book, reading out random sentences and asking if this was really something he was enjoying.

Patricia put the fish away in the fridge and sat down heavily on the sofa, closing her eyes and trying to breathe calmly [Sally read aloud, from what Jack recognised was an early Ivy scene]. But, as she opened her eyes again, she immediately noticed a smudge in the top-lefthand corner of her bay window. It hadn't been there yesterday, she was quite sure. She had been looking forward to a relaxing evening in her own company at last, but Ivy's remarks about her dated dressing gown had stayed with her. And now she found that she couldn't rest until the smudge on the window had been removed.

'Are you really telling me you've been reading this nonsense all week?' Sally asked her husband, stupefied. 'Since when have you been into window-cleaning?'
She picked up another section at random.

It was only as the bolder light of the afternoon gave way to the tepid tones of early evening, after the day's chores and errands and outings had been despatched and her simple dinner for one consumed . . . only then did Patricia sometimes become vulnerable to a certain wistful melancholy. It was, she knew, a feeling that the simple pleasures of an easy companionship might well dispel. But at such times she consoled herself with the bitter fruit of her own experience: the knowledge that a life wrongly shared is a far lonelier proposition than a solitary life lived on one's own terms. And gamely she would rise and reach for a book to read or a disc to play, reminding herself that her choice in such matters was hers now – and hers alone.

Jack had just read this bit, but he was moved again by this brave spirit who had had to learn the pleasures and perils of independence so late in life. 'Oh my God, will she just get to the point already!' said Sally, who was a sucker for any book with *Death, Die* or *Murder* in the title. Also *Kill* or *Killing*.
Now she shuffled the pages, and dealt again:

In the bottom of the fireproof metal case where Victor kept all their share certificates, Patricia noticed for the first time a thin sheet of paper, folded neatly in half. She picked it up and saw at once that it was a note to Victor, written in faded ink in a confident female hand. She did not need to read the whole message to know that the author was someone who knew him very intimately. And she did not need to read a single word to know that the author was not herself.

At this, Jack lost it. He wrenched the paperback out of her wrist, and stomped out of the room. 'Oh no!' called out Sally, her voice thick with satire. 'Not a spoiler, was it?'

'Don't be so fucking stupid,' snarled Jack, who had slammed the door behind him, and was now paging furiously through the book to see how much of it she'd ruined.

That afternoon, Jack and Sally and Abby and Tilly went for a dinosaur walk on the beach. It was led by a fully qualified and extremely passionate palaeontologist, who was full of dino facts, several of them actually quite interesting, and who helped them to identify rocks and crystals and fossils on the beach.

'Now, has anyone seen the film *Jurassic Park*?' asked the palaeontologist.

Every arm went up.

'Well: IT SHOULD HAVE BEEN CALLED *CRETACEOUS PARK!*' she shouted, eyes ablaze.

Jack smiled gently. He couldn't help thinking of Patricia's remark to herself after listening to another of Gordon's interminable lectures on Perpendicular church architecture:

Though he was quite lacking in the ability to assess his audience's level of interest in a topic, it was hard not to warm to someone who cared so much about their subject. What was pedantry after all, but unrequited passion?

Jack's daughters were obsessed with crystals, and ran back and forth to their instructor with endless samples of promising-looking sparkly bits of rock. Sally found a mollusc fossil, and

Tilly turned up a fragment of an ancient shark fin. Abby trumped them both with the find of a rare ammonite, full of crystal. Even the palaeontologist looked impressed. 'No one's touched or seen that for probably 115 million years!' she said excitedly.

Not to be outdone, Jack unearthed a dark lump with an interesting cross-stitched pattern. Calcite? Fool's gold? A rare sliver of plesiosaurus bone? 'Now *that*,' said the palaeontologist, 'comes from over the clifftop.'

'Isn't that where the biggest fossils are found?' said Jack eagerly.

'Higher than that,' she said. 'This piece is one hundred per cent . . . *tarmac.*'

'Well done, babe!' said Sally. 'You've uncovered a rare bit of . . . pure road!'

The others all laughed. And though their laughter was directed at him, Jack saw it was a kind of embrace, warm and inclusive. He threw back his head, and laughed long and hard at Jack too.

FRIDAY

On the last full day of their holiday, Jack was up and out early for a promised session of jet-skiing with the boys.

'Where you been all week?' said the one called 'Nitro'. 'We ain't seen you since the cave-dive.'

'Oh just chillaxing,' said Jack casually.

'Back under the thumb, are we?' said the one called 'Pog'. He bared his teeth as he smirked, and Jack saw that they were crooked and stained.

'It's a fine thumb to be under,' said Jack.

'S'pose you gotta say that,' said Pog. 'Don't think I could be with someone who stopped me being myself.'

'Certainly I find that I am *notoriously uxorious* these days,' said Jack, to his own bafflement.

In the third and final section of the curtain magnolia book, Patricia Porlock discovers a letter from one Vanessa Pritchard, an office manager in Victor's firm and evidently his lover for several years, right up until his sudden demise.

This was the development that Jack had been dreading. Gordon had made claims on Patricia's future, and Ivy had sought to monopolise her present, but Vanessa stood to destabilise Patricia's very sense of herself, her memories, her identity: her *past*.

Victor had been a fusspot and a hypochondriac and an idle chauvinist, it was true. But at least he had been these things *for her*, exclusively, or so she had assumed.

And indeed, in his crap little way, he had at least tried to make some acknowledgement of what she did for him:

When they were entertaining, and his guests took a moment to compliment Victor on the meal or the wine or the decor of their Bayswater home, he always made a point of passing the credit on to Patricia. 'It is I who should be giving thanks – Patricia's the one who made it all happen,' he would say. 'No wonder I am notoriously uxorious.'

He did it all for show, of course, and as soon as the guests had left he would slump in front of the television with a Scotch and not another word to his wife, while she fussed around clearing the table and loading the dishwasher and reorganising the fridge and sweeping the carpet (she couldn't *vacuum* at night – he said the noise upset him) and all the hundred-and-one other little invisible jobs that go with running a home and keeping up appearances in a world – Victor's world – where the wrong choice of lampshade could apparently scupper an entire round of 'seed funding'.

Out in the kitchen, wielding dustpan and brush, Patricia would always reflect on the guests' compliments and Victor's latest little speech of thanks, comparing them with previous efforts for sincerity and originality. She took pleasure in the thought of another evening successfully catered for, took pride in the praise for her tasteful home. *These are my crumbs*, she thought as she swept. *Mine alone*.

But now, here comes Vanessa Pritchard to shit over all that. In a tense meeting at a local patisserie, Patricia finally comes face to face with her husband's lover.

Vanessa Pritchard was a buxom, purposeful-looking woman with a resolute chin and a markedly frank gaze. She was, Patricia recognised, the sort of woman that many a man might go for: confident in her physicality, boldly expressive of her wants and desires, and effortlessly, if a touch provocatively, stylish. Where Patricia had been passive, Vanessa was assertive. Where Patricia had always dressed to melt pleasantly into the passing scene, Vanessa dressed to turn heads. Where Patricia had always played a compliant and supportive role, Vanessa demanded to be wooed and won. She was, thought Patricia, the sort of woman she had always found terrifying.

Jack thought: *Why doesn't she just deck the bitch?* Yet again, he marvelled at Patricia's superhuman powers of forbearance – the way she managed to find compassion in her heart for her heartless love rival.

In short, each was everything that the other was not. And in realising this, Patricia realised too that she could not really bring herself to hate Vanessa. Vanessa wasn't a superior version of herself, she was her photographic negative. Victor had found someone to fill the gaps in their marriage; and though she hadn't consciously looked to do the same, she had every sympathy with his impulse.

Looking at the deep red of Vanessa's long and perfectly manicured nails, all Patricia could feel was: pity. Pity for Victor, pity for Vanessa, pity for herself. What an absurd and tedious game the three of them had played – a game from which there could be no winners, only a scramble for consolations.

So far, so magnanimous. Only what's this now? What's this doc Vanessa is pulling out of a brown envelope? Of *course*! The evil cow is laying claim to the flat!

Not content with stealing her husband and revealing Patricia's entire twenty-three-year marriage to have been a giant sham, Vanessa now wants to steal her very home from her!

SATURDAY AGAIN

Saturday, the day of their departure, found Jack skulking in the loo, desperate for some space to finish the magnolia curtain book.

Whenever something mega-dramatic happened, the author had this funny way of turning away from the action . . . and doing another of her funny little fishmonger scenes. It must be a way of keeping you wondering how Patricia's feeling and what her next move will be, he thought. Not only that, Jack realised with a sudden flash of inspiration, but the conversations about the fish always ended up offering a little clue about which way things were going.

One time, for instance, the fishmonger offered to trim all the cartilage off her skate wings. Some customers found it helpful, he said, as they didn't have the knife skills or perhaps the right tool for the job. But Patricia, who wasn't lacking in either department, said she'd be happy to do it herself. At first Jack had thought she was being a bit stroppy, but now he realised that this scene – which comes just before the famous letter to Ivy – was a sign of Patricia learning to stand up for herself.

So here she was at Le Comptoir de l'Océan again, this time asking Grégoire the best way to cook sole.

She was looking forward to him waxing ecstatic about one of his elaborate French sauces, waving his arms around theatrically as he sliced and diced imaginary ingredients and stirred and seasoned them in a rich if equally imaginary *jus*. But instead he simply raised a finger. 'With sole, simplicity is all,' he pronounced. 'Butter, lemon, parsley, nothing more! Just as my wife says.'

Patricia couldn't help smiling. 'So when it comes to cooking fish, Grégoire, you of all people . . . defer to *your wife*?'

'In this, as in all things, *chère madame*,' pronounced Grégoire again, finger still pointed skywards. There was a twinkle in his eye, but it did not somehow belie the seriousness of his words.

Patricia, like Jack, had needed to look up the word 'uxorious' (though of course she used her *Concise Oxford English Dictionary*, whereas Jack had crassly resorted to Google). It turned out to mean 'excessively fond of or submissive to one's wife'.

How strange, Patricia mused, to see that word 'excessively' in the definition – as if the dictionary itself could not resist reminding men of the foolishness of paying too much attention to their wives.

It was a definition, thought Jack, of which 'Termite' or 'Nitro' might have been proud. And the funny thing was, it turned out that there was no real equivalent for the opposite – no word for a woman silly enough to like or obey her husband too much. 'That's just how it should be though, innit?' as 'Pogo' or 'Spum' would no doubt have said.

Back in the patisserie, as she waited for Vanessa to return from her nose-powdering, Patricia mused on this odd word and its meanings for her life.

I was, if not excessively fond, then certainly excessively obedient to Victor, she thought. I indulged all his funny little habits, his foibles and phobias, kept the show on the road in the background so he could play the big man. And in return, he spent his nights away in hotel rooms, playing the fool with this . . . *brassy bombshell*.

Fuck, thought Jack, she is mad. Coming from her, this was fighting talk. And quite right too. No doubt Victor had sat up in bed with Vanessa, telling her what an unadventurous little mouse his wife was. But even a mouse has her limits. And the flat – whose bestowal on her Patricia saw now was a gesture of both confession and penance on Victor's part – was *hers*. She wasn't going to give it up without a fight.

Patricia stood up, and started to gather her things. She had money enough, perhaps, to fight Vanessa's legal claims. But she didn't want things to go that far.

'Vanessa,' she said evenly. 'You must understand that everything that Victor had to give you – you've taken already.'

'We used to go to that flat a lot,' said Vanessa. 'It was virtually my home at times.'

Patricia stifled a gasp on hearing this. It was painful, and unexpected. And yet, of course, it was logical, obvious. The flat had been Victor's sanctuary before it was hers.

'You were a kept woman,' said Patricia grimly. 'I'm afraid they don't tend to have too many rights in the long run.'

'I've taken advice,' Vanessa persisted mechanically, extending an obstinate chin. 'We can let the courts decide.'

Another thought seized Patricia. 'But you can't have been the only one? Otherwise why wouldn't Victor let you live there all the time?'

'I know my rights,' she said, ignoring this awkward point. 'I've taken advice.'

'Have many more of you were there?' persisted Patricia with forensic glee, quite unlike herself.

'This is about *me* and what I'm entitled to,' said Vanessa fiercely.

Patricia ignored this. 'Have you thought about finding them all and launching a class action? I could perhaps help – I still have some of Victor's old diaries and things. He liked to write everything down long-hand, you know – never trusted computers.'

Jack was pissing himself. Over the course of his increasingly fascinated journey through the magnolia curtain book, he had come to admire Patricia, to respect her, to feel sorry for her and to root for her. Hell, he had even come to fancy her a little bit. (Vanessa too, and quite a lot, if he was honest.) But now it turned out she was a fucking comedian too!

'Come on, love!' Sally knocked on the toilet door. 'Let's get this show on the road! Come and help me pack the car!'

He had three pages left, and Patricia had just booked a consultation with a respected local firm who specialised in bespoke curtains. She was tempted by the beautiful fabrics and the traditional decorative finish that a goblet or deep double-pleat design would no doubt offer; but then again, one of the new eyelet styles with its lovely metallic finish would add a contemporary flourish to her space. Decisions, decisions!

Just then, as Jack emerged from the loo, one of his girls came rushing up the stairs, her face a picture of teary distress. 'Daddy, Daddy!' she cried. 'I can't find my fossil!!'

Jack tucked in his shirt, and applied himself to the search for the ancient mollusc.

'You know what, Abby?' he said, crouching down to her eye level. 'You don't look a bit like your sister!' Abby, who had never thought otherwise, looked confused.

He had three pages left. But they would keep.

ACKNOWLEDGEMENTS

I'm very grateful to all the publishers and competitions who have found a space for my stories, including Flash 500 ('In here'); *Pithead Chapel* ('Active and passive voice'); *The Fiction Pool* ('Near miss'); *Reflex Fiction* ('Listing to port'); Retreat West ('Foods of love'); *Riptide Journal* ('Ella G in a Country Churchyard); *Ellipsis Zine* ('The paths of the great lovers cross at Victoria station'); *Lucent Dreaming* ('The virtual writer') and Leicester Writes ('Our special words for things'). I'm especially grateful to Simon Webster, Chief Polisher of *The Cabinet of Heed* ('Infinite rainbows', 'First world problems'), who has published several of my stories.

A very big thank you to everyone who has read and fed back on these stories too, including: Eve Brotzel, Isla Brotzel, Adam Cooper, Mark Drew, Jenny Fielder, Christian Lapper, Matt Kendrick, Rob Pointer, Sarah Riley, Emily Shelley and CM Taylor. Special thanks to Martin, Debs, John, Christy, Ash and everyone connected with the Conway writers' group.

More important shout-outs: To Ger Nichol, my agent, for plucking me out of her inbox when I was working as a waitress in a cocktail bar (so to speak). To Moira Forsyth, my editor, for repeatedly saving me from myself with her shrewd assessments and patient care. To Nathan Burton, for his witty cover. To Rebecca Wojturska, for her painstaking proofing. To Ceris, Nicola and everyone at Sandstone.

To Alex Woolf, writing mentor and friend, without whom I would never have got to here.

Love and thanks and everything to Eve, Isla, Poppy and Huw. You guys.

www.sandstonepress.com

 facebook.com/SandstonePress/

@SandstonePress